Death Rattle

Carter Pugh

Carter Pugh Writes LLC

Cover design by Donato Pizzuti

Edited by Melisa Graham

Published by Carter Pugh Writes LLC

ISBN: 9798988552079

To Murph, who said I had lightning in a bottle.

A death rattle is a crackling, wet sound that is heard at varying levels with each breath. It may sound as if the person is "drowning" or choking. It can also sound like a soft or low moan as the person struggles to breathe. The dying person is usually unaware of the noisy breathing and is not disturbed by it.

The death rattle signals that death is very near.

PROLOGUE

I didn't think I'd ever been this excited about anything in my life. Anxious energy buzzed through my whole body. This was it. Step one to making my dreams come true. Literally.

The first dream started about six months ago. I'd woken up sobbing, wanting to go back. The way I felt in the dream was like coming home, like taking my first real breath, like coming back to life after walking among the dead. In this dream, the world around me was dark, inky black, swirling with red mist. The darkness enveloped me like a second skin, like a lover, forming to the curves of my body and sending pleasurable chills throughout. I breathed in the red mist deep into my lungs like a drug.

Euphoria.

I'd had the same dream over and over since that first night. The last one had added something new. I'd met someone in the dream: a wraith-like creature, shadowed in black. I couldn't remember their face, but what they'd told me was branded onto my soul. They told me they could give me anything I desired, that they had the power to give me everything I'd ever wanted—I just had to do a few favors for them.

The first thing was to kill a specific person. I'd never killed before, so my lack of restraint surprised me. Until now, I didn't think myself capable. But when I plotted how I would do it, I felt a rush of excitement, not revulsion. It was intoxicating.

"I want to stay here," I told the wraith. "I want to be adored and powerful, and I want the person I love to love me in return, wholly and forever." They promised me all this and more.

The craving for this place and the life they promised me was driving me insane. It was all-consuming—an itch I couldn't scratch, a hunger I couldn't sate. My everyday life became meaningless. I never doubted this dark stranger or the realness of the dreams. It's like when you hear something that is indisputably true. Your soul recognizes it; it hits you at your core.

If I was successful, I would get everything I'd ever wanted. Everything that I'd always deserved. But first, I had to snuff out one insignificant life.

I'd made my decision, and my resolve was unwavering.

As I unlocked the back door of a dark apartment, walked a few quick steps, and quietly opened the door to a dark bedroom, a calm washed over me. I walked resolutely to the bed where a woman lay sleeping. I raised a hunting knife right over her heart … and then stepped over the precipice, embracing the amazing life waiting for me. As I shoved the knife through her chest, breaking through her sternum and ribcage, the warm rush of her blood sprayed over my hand, and I felt a wet warmth splash across my face. As the blood dripped into my eye, the dark room was cast in a red tinge.

I looked down as the whites of her eyes widened with shock and fear as she died silently. Elation and triumph filled my body. *I did it.*

It unleashed me, and I became untethered and unbelievable.

CHAPTER 1

Halfway between dreaming and waking, I jolted up, painfully aware of an intense throbbing in my lower abdomen. It hurt and felt good at the same time. My heart was racing, and I was slightly sweaty and out of breath.

What the hell was that?

The memory of deep-green eyes staring into mine, heated touches, and colliding body parts sent another exquisitely pleasant spasm through my pelvis. Did I just have a sex dream and wake up in the middle of an orgasm? Was that a thing?

I knew men could have wet dreams, but I'd never heard of a woman having something similar. Sure, I'd had sexy dreams before but not to *completion*. They'd just left me aroused and unfulfilled when I woke in the morning.

I reached for my cell phone on my nightstand and in the process knocked off the necklace my mom had given me. I thanked the wine gods that I'd remembered to take it off last night before going to bed. Otherwise, the chain might be a kinked mess. I unhooked the phone from the charger and typed "can a woman orgasm in their sleep?" in the search bar.

"Holy shit!" I scream-whispered and jack-knifed to a seated position in my bed.

This was a real thing. It was called a nocturnal orgasm and, apparently, was completely normal. How the hell was that normal? My core still ached from the aftermath.

"What a way to wake up," I said to my ever-empty bedroom. My room was huge, as I had the loft bedroom upstairs. It had a black sectional couch where I liked to nap and read books, a small TV, and a king-sized bed with black silk bedding. My walls were painted a dull shell white, and I had decorated them with pictures of my mom, dad, and friends I'd met since I moved to the city.

I rolled over to find the book I'd been reading wedged underneath a pillow. The culprit of my sex dream, I supposed. Guess that was the last time I read another book about the fae and their steamy sexcapades before going to bed. Maybe it was a sign that I needed to get laid … or take matters into my own hands.

I'd been so tired lately, which was weird because I'd felt so energized just a few months ago around my birthday. But now, I was depleted. I'd been so busy from work and school that I'd been completely on autopilot. I didn't feel like dating. I hated meeting new people—well, new people that were potential bedfellows.

Dating in your thirties was like being on the worst interview of your life with someone new every few days. It was a torturous spin cycle ranging from stage-five clingers to hit-it-and-quit-it ghosters. Even if you both felt that elusive "spark," it normally ended with an "I'm just not emotionally ready to commit to someone right now." Like, in our thirties, whole ass adults couldn't even commit to having a regular fuck buddy. I think I'd probably settle for that at this point: a nice, clean person who wanted to have sex exclusively with me, no emotional intimacy necessary. That had become my best-case scenario, and it pretty much blew. That's why my nights were currently occupied by me, myself, and my sexy book boyfriends. Well, that and now sexy dreams and nocturnal orgasms. I'd just add that to the list of why I was still the weirdest person I knew.

I was stuck in a rut, and obviously, my body was trying to tell me something. "Well, bitch," I said to my vagina, "we are in our grinding phase—no, not that kind of grinding! Calm the hell down! We have real work to do, a career to start, and bills to pay."

I patted the old girl like a boy you'd put in the friend zone, yawned, stretched, kicked off my covers, picked up my mom's necklace, and placed it back on my nightstand. Then I clicked on the TV to listen to the morning news as I prepared for my day.

"Shit, this floor is freezing!" I said again to the vacant room. I had a habit of talking to myself. Sometimes I almost felt like someone was watching me, like hidden cameras were recording me like the guy on *The Truman Show*. Stop talking to yourself and buy some rugs immediately, I thought. I'd never gotten used to how cold my condo's floors were. I'd grown up in a house with carpet everywhere, even in the bathrooms. This was the first time I had wood and concrete underfoot, and I still wasn't used to the cold shock to my feet. "Purchase rugs and slippers" went on my mental to-do list.

In my bathroom, a room bigger than my bedroom growing up, I relieved myself and started getting ready for the day. The bathroom had two sinks, a huge walk-in shower, a giant bathtub, and a small closet for the toilet. The floor was a gray and white marble tile, and the walls were painted the same shell white as my bedroom.

I felt lighter as I slowly woke up. My eyes cleared from the blurriness of sleep. My dark brown hair that resembled a bird's nest looked like I'd actually experienced all that sexiness I'd been dreaming about. If only. I'd never even brought a date back here. No one I'd met since moving to Uptown Charlotte was worth a second date, let alone a bedroom visit. My normally bright green eyes were glassy, courtesy of that third glass of wine I had before falling asleep. "Note to self," I said into the mirror, "maybe drink less, Clarke. Or, you know, maybe not. It's currently your only vice."

My skin looked pale but with a bit of olive tone, which was good since I worked too much to get an actual tan, and I usually avoided the sun anyway. I was a touch too vain to let anything age my face. Turning thirty had me upping my skincare routine and purchasing sunscreen by the gallons. I lathered that shit on daily.

As my body automatically performed my morning routine, my mind started running through all the homework I needed to finish before tomorrow. The fall semester had just begun, and my professors liked to bombard us with heavy work on day one.

I had two semesters left, and then I'd finally graduate. I was finishing my degree in history. I know, I know—I was thirty and finishing my four-year degree. But, hey, at least I was finishing it, right? I'd dropped out of college in my sophomore year when my mom's illness had taken a turn for the worse. Seeing her wither away in front of my eyes had diminished something in me. It was like I couldn't proceed with my future if she didn't have one anymore.

Before she'd gotten sick, my mom was the most vivacious person I knew. She was magnetic and drew everyone in. She'd made me feel like my capabilities were endless.

I'd always had trouble making friends. Most kids thought I was strange; I grew up in a small town where being artistic meant weird and being different felt like a crime. I had trouble communicating with kids my age, often gravitating toward an older and more mature crowd who found my behavior entertaining instead of off-putting. When I wasn't being ignored by the various cliques at school, I was bullied or picked on for thinking I was too good for the kids my age or the fact that I read all the time but still managed to have poor grades. Many times, I would run into my mom's arms crying as soon as I got home from school, telling her story after story of how lonely I was or how someone had said something unkind to me.

When I got nervous, I felt awkward and would stumble over my words, or I would act out in class to get laughs and attention. The kids liked me in those moments, but the teachers didn't. In elementary school, I ended up in the principal's office weekly. When they'd call my mom, she would arrive calmly with a warm smile and talk the teacher or principal into letting me off with a warning. My pediatrician had even suggested I'd be put on Ritalin, a drug for ADHD, to help regulate my moods and classroom outbursts. Mom refused and didn't take me back to that doctor again. She took my side always. She said the doctor was confusing my uniqueness for a disorder and that I didn't need medicine, just time and space to be myself. She was the only one who truly understood me and assured me that I was perfect just the way I was.

I only felt secure when my mom was near me. She would sometimes come to school and eat lunch with me. Those days were my favorite. All the kids would flock to sit with us at lunch as if I had a celebrity sitting with me, and for the whole rest of the day, I'd be treated like I was someone special too. The shine would always wear off though, and things would return to normal the next day.

My mom was my light in the dark of every bad day. She never looked at me with pity but would comfort me with her perfect words. She was my best friend, my other half. Without her, I felt knocked off kilter and I didn't think I would ever feel balanced again.

When I dropped out of college, I knew Mom would never want me to put my life on hold for her, but I had already started to fall behind after her diagnosis and decided to withdraw before it reflected in my GPA.

After she passed away, I took a nanny position and started making good money. I got used to the income quickly, thoughts of school were left behind. Then my dad became ill and died shortly after my mom, so I inherited our two-story home in the middle of the woods in rural eastern North Carolina. I'd tried to keep the house; it was my last connection to my family. It was paid off but still required lots of maintenance as it was an old home. I began fixing things myself when they broke, thanks to YouTube tutorials. I taught myself how to cook and entertained myself by reading to escape the loneliness I felt when I was home. I'd stopped painting though; the act of it reminded me of my mom and the joy on her face when she saw me creating. Instead, I threw myself into work. The woman I nannied for was all too grateful for the extra hours I requested. In my early twenties, I had to maintain a home full of memories and sorrow I wanted to escape. I had no friends and no social life at that point, so I helped the family I worked for, taking their life on as my own.

After a few years, I started feeling like a ghost haunting that old house, my soul crumbling like the house around me. I decided to sell the house and the land and move. My mom had never spoken about her family much, and my dad was estranged from his. Something about a family schism that happened when my parents got married. Apparently, his family disliked my mother, who was a saint, so I always assumed they were horrible people. So with no family to leave behind, I decided to leave the town and its lingering ghosts.

About a year ago, the sale of the house had gone through, and I'd made enough for a down payment on a condo in Charlotte, in the heart of the city known to the locals as Uptown. I'd originally thought that they were just trying to be trendy or stand out by calling it that until one of the locals explained that it was a way to promote a more positive, upbeat image of the city's center. And it actually does sit at a higher elevation than the rest of the city, so it literally is *Up*town.

I'd moved to the city, found a new nanny position, and started going back to school. I'd always loved history class in school and thought maybe it'd be a fun subject to teach. Even though my school experience had been less than perfect, I thought after everything I'd been through, I'd be able to help kids like me. Kids that might need a bit more attention and understanding than what I was given. So I'd enrolled in an online/hybrid program.

With my new nanny position, I made enough income to afford my mortgage and utilities but just barely, so I got a roommate to help with my expenses.

Things were looking up. Those years after my parents' deaths felt like a dream I'd woken up from. That person, that ghost who had haunted my childhood home didn't even feel like me anymore. She was lost, and while I didn't quite have my life figured out, I had a path now, goals. I owned a home and struggled to pay bills, like most adults my age, while working toward a future.

The condo was peaceful that morning. My roommate, Heather, was gone, and I didn't think she'd slept at home last night, but it was hard to tell. Heather had thin, mousy brown hair that dusted her collar bone, gray-green forlorn eyes, and was so slim that she'd felt frail when I awkwardly greeted her with a hug the first time we met.

Heather was always so quiet and kept to herself despite me constantly nagging her to hang out. I was really hoping she wasn't here last night after my weird sex dream likely had me making embarrassing sounds. I've been told I'm not a quiet sleeper—I talk, snore, kick, and now moan. Oh god, who does that?! Me, I did that now.

My face heated in remembrance of the super-real-feeling dream and the sexy eyes that reminded me of the emerald hue of the ocean off the coast of Florida. I'd only been there once but had never seen anything so beautiful. I was used to the murky Carolina coastal waters. While still beautiful in their own way, they were nothing as magical as the ones in the Sunshine State.

Shaking my head to reset and clear my mind, I got dressed in my normal nanny uniform: a pair of black sweatpants, a kid-friendly band tee, and my favorite pair of red and white chucks. I used to wear my mom's necklace every day without fail, but last week, one of the kids had tried to yank it from my neck. Kids are often attracted to bright and shiny things, so I got it, but if they had broken it, I would've been livid. It was irreplaceable. After she'd given it to me, she'd cautioned me to take good care of it. Something about it being a family heirloom that went back centuries. So now when I go to work, I leave it safely on my nightstand beside my bed.

I glimpsed a scene on TV that stopped me dead in my tracks. I grabbed the remote and turned the sound up: "Experts are suggesting this global phenomenon could be caused by global warming, while others speculate that it's a widespread art concept from artisans around the world. Whatever it is, world leaders are urging caution but assure us that there is no reason to panic."

I immersed myself in the images flashing by on the screen: hot pink and electric blue oceans; vibrant, bulbous, architectural shapes that seemed to sprout from dilapidated buildings; and auras in the sky that looked like mirrors to another world. It struck me speechless. Whatever this was, artistic expression or a crazy unnatural wonder, it was beautiful.

Glancing at the clock next to the TV, I sighed heavily. I could not be late again. Global crisis or not, I had to get on with my day. I clicked the TV off and headed downstairs. Luckily, the family I worked for lived a couple blocks away, so the walk over wouldn't take long. I had sold my car to save money when I moved to Charlotte and was thankful for a job that did not require me to drive. Walking was like meditation for me.

I walked outside and cursed myself for forgetting to at least check if Heather was home before leaving. I shot her a quick text to tell her I was headed to work and that I'd see her later. I never wanted to be rude, and I hated leaving without saying bye. I'm sure she didn't care either way, but it mattered to me. I wanted us to be friends. When we'd first met, I'd felt an instant kinship, as if our scarred souls could see one another and felt safe in proximity. The pain behind her eyes was hard to miss since I recognized the haunting gaze as a mirror to my own.

I turned to lock the door behind me. Glancing up at the exterior of our building, a smile broke across my face. I loved my condo. It was part of a big industrial-looking building in Uptown filled with several condo apartments. Our condo was two stories with a vaulted ceiling, which made it appear bigger than it really was, and it was perfect for me and my roommate. It had almost separate living areas for her and me. We each had an en suite bathroom, so if we didn't want to be bothered, or in her case if she didn't want to be social, we could basically exist wholly apart from one another. We did, however, share a living room space where sometimes she would join me when I watched my favorite trashy TV shows.

My mind was clear as I started up the hill of my street to the main road. Smiling, I walked by my favorite landmark—I called it Narnia. It was a collection of tree-like shrubs that had grown together but left a path in the middle that appeared to go on forever. I'd once ventured inside before and found the end just came to a stop where the shrubs joined again. Disappointedly boring.

Ever since I'd first read about Lucy finding another world through a wardrobe in her uncle's house and going on terrible and exciting adventures, I'd longed to do the same. Even at thirty, I yearned to believe in magic, maybe not the fairytale version, but how there was a vibe and energy that lived in all things—like the magic in the way a bumble bee scientifically couldn't fly, but it didn't know that, so it flew anyway. As a kid, I'd fantasized about being a witch in real life. I still thought that having magical powers and manipulating the elements could be possible. After all, magic was just science that hadn't been discovered yet. Just a hundred years ago, most people would have said going to the moon could only be done with magic. But scientists never limited themselves by what most people would say was possible. That's how I wanted to live: like there were endless possibilities. The future was unknown, and anything was possible. If I limited my thinking to believing everything was black and white and put my life in a box, I would never have that magical, limitless life. I didn't want to live in black and white, not anymore.

I had always felt an odd sense of other about myself, like there was a corner of my mind that I couldn't quite get to that held the answer as to why I was different. Like when you see a shadow out of the corner of your eye, but when you turn to look, there is nothing there. I was just waiting for a cat with a crescent moon scar to show up and say, "Hey, it's you! You're this! Haven't you always known?" Or for some long-lost family member to call me up and tell me I was some foreign princess of a small country and they'd been searching for me. Then I'd understand my life, like finding the final puzzle piece hidden somewhere—that one thing that would make it all fit and explain everything. Then maybe I wouldn't be in this funk feeling alone and lost.

Gosh, Clarke, stop being so depressing, I thought. You have friends now; you aren't alone, dumbass. Friends I've been ignoring for a few weeks now. As if on cue, my phone buzzed in my pocket. Alison, my best friend, had texted again. Her big smile peered back at me as her photo popped up on my phone screen.

I felt terrible ignoring her, but I was busy and didn't feel like meeting up with our friends after work. I just wanted to cocoon and be by myself for a few more days until I could shake this funk off. So I sent her a message back promising we would hang out next weekend and turned the sound off. I really missed my best friend and "the crew" as she called our friend group. I just didn't want them to see me all depressed and weird.

They'd met me six months ago at the height of my I'm-going-to-be-positive-and-win-at-life phase. I wanted them to still see me as that girl. That's who I wanted to be, not the sad Clarke I'd been the twenty-eight years before I'd moved to the city. I wasn't her anymore; I had to shake her off before anyone saw her. She was supposed to be gone. I thought I'd left that side of me behind, and I was determined for that to be the case.

I always felt so frustrated when these moments of depression washed over me. It was a creeping feeling that crawled up from the depths and took hold of everything good and peaceful inside me. What's worse is that I often struggled to find its source. Was it as simple as my failed dating life? Was I burnt out from school and work? Could it really be the pain of losing my mom, ebbing and flowing, sometimes becoming cripplingly painful even after years of grieving? No matter how long I thought about it, nothing I came up with felt like the catalyst, so I would just carry on hoping it'd go away. Most times, if I stayed busy, it would sluff off like it'd never happened.

Arriving at work, I set out about my day with the two kids I nannied. I enjoyed working there for the most part. The kids were great; I loved them. The parents were a little weird. After work last week, they'd pulled me into a meeting in their home office to reprimand me for letting the little boy (age two) play with his four-year-old sister's dolls. I was shocked at the implication that I had done something wrong by allowing the little guy to play with a "girl's toy." Sometimes you don't realize people's values until something like this happens. They obviously were way off the mark with what my values were, but I was out of there as soon as I graduated and got a job in my field. I just had to keep my head above water until then, keep my mouth shut, and keep collecting my paycheck. I felt sorry for their son though. It's just a toy. How could they be so threatened by a toy?

The day went by quickly. I made lunch, took the kids to the park, and did some dishes while the kids watched TV. Their mom returned home, and after saying goodbye to the kids, I grabbed my things and opened the back door to leave.

As I stepped out into the crisp autumn air, the wind picked up, twirling the fallen leaves into perfect dancing circles. I loved the fall in the South when the air finally stopped feeling like you were breathing in thick pea soup. The cooler air made my soul feel alive and at ease. It had already started getting darker earlier. The sun was setting as I made my way back to my condo. A warm grin spread across my face as I admired the pinks and oranges of the sunset.

As I walked down the hill, I noticed the streetlights were out. Great, the power was out again. Someone was always wrecking into our transformer since we lived off a busy road. We would sometimes lose power for days while the city repaired the damage.

When I arrived home, I shucked my shoes off and walked barefoot toward the coat closet by the back door where we kept the candles and flashlights. Holding my hands out in front of me so my clumsy ass didn't smash into anything, my hand finally connected with the closet door handle. I reached in and felt around until I found everything I needed.

As I passed by my roommate's room, I knocked. "Heather, are you home?" Her door cracked open, and I stepped inside the room. It was cold and smelled pungent. The smell assaulted my nostrils and made me curl my nose, my body's automatic attempt to block the stench. Heather usually kept things neat and tidy, but her room now smelled stale, like something I couldn't really identify.

"Sorry to barge in," I apologized in a hushed tone, "but the power's out again, and I'm just—"

I slipped on something wet and landed on my ass. Hard.

"What the fuck!"

I'd landed in a damp puddle, and my candles had tumbled from my arms. Ugh, was the smell vomit? Was Heather sick? If I was sitting in a pool of old puke, I was going to puke too.

The flashlight I'd been holding had crashed on the floor. Turning on from the impact, it cast a light in the dark room toward Heather's bed, illuminating the pool of whatever I was sitting in. It spread from her bed to where I sat with my legs sprawled.

Something sticky and red trickled down from the mattress and covered the floor below. With alarming clarity, I realized what I was looking at. Blood. I was staring at blood, like a shit ton of blood. I shifted my gaze slowly from the floor up to where the light ended. My breath caught in my throat. An arm was hanging limply off the bed in an unnatural position. A coldness swept through my veins, and shock and nausea took root.

CHAPTER 2

I knew the blood was Heather's. I knew that was her arm hanging off her bed. I knew the tacky substance smearing into my sweatpants was blood, not vomit, and I also knew I needed to get up. I understood that, but I couldn't focus, couldn't think around a loud screeching sound. Had someone pulled the fire alarm? If it would just stop, I could get my head together. I needed to call someone. I needed to do something. "Get up, Clarke," I said. "Get the fuck up! Move!"

Reality crashed into me like a bucket of ice-cold water poured over my head. The screeching sound wasn't an alarm. It was me; I was screaming.

I needed to stop. My ears were hot, and my vision started to blur. I needed to get a grip on myself and the situation around me.

My mother's gentle words sounded so clearly in my mind that she could've been standing right there speaking to me in that moment, reminding me of the time she taught me how to breathe to calm myself down when I got too upset or too angry. "Breathe in slowly, breathe out slowly," she said. "Breathe in slowly, breathe out slowly. Big deep breath. Let it out."

As my screaming quieted, I wiped my hands, sticky with Heather's blood, on my now-ruined band tee and used the spot of clean floor near me to push up into a standing position.

I grabbed the flashlight and searched for my phone. Luckily, it had fallen out of my pocket onto a section of the floor not covered in blood. Well, it was clean, but the screen was now cracked, thanks to the hardness of the concrete floors. I swiped up to unlock it and dialed 911. The dispatcher answered after a few rings and asked what my emergency was.

"Um, Heather, my roommate—" I choked a little on the words I'd tried to say. I cleared my throat and continued, "I just found my roommate. She's … I think she's dead."

After they asked for my address, they told me that an officer would be there shortly and to stay on the line with them until the officer reached me. They instructed me not to move anything or leave the premises. Yeah, no worries there. I was basically standing like a statue in Heather's bedroom, frozen with … fear? Grief? Shock? I didn't even know. What I knew was that my roommate was likely dead. Did she hurt herself? I didn't know if she was depressed, but do you ever really know that about someone? The dark thoughts kept coming as I stood there holding the flashlight limp in my hand.

Staring into the darkness in a daze, my heart started racing, and alarming new thoughts formed: "If she didn't do this to herself, who did? Did someone kill Heather? Oh shit, if they did, are they still here? Fuck … fuck!" Just as I began to hyperventilate, I heard a knock at the door and almost jumped out of my skin. A voice then announced that officers were entering the premises in response to a 911 call. "We're back here," I croaked.

As the first responders began their work, I thought back to the one and only time Heather and I had gone out together. I had begged her to come out with me. She could be a little reclusive, and even though she'd been my roommate for a few months, I barely knew anything about her.

The bar, Murph's, had been loud and packed when we got there. We followed the crowd's energy straight to the dance floor, or rather the cleared area bar patrons had co-opted as a dance floor. After working up a thirst, I told Heather it was time for drinks. "Grab me a rum and coke?" she yelled through the haze and noise. I headed to the bar and squeezed in an opening between two people. I wasn't always good at getting a bartender's attention, but ever since I moved Uptown, I'd become a regular here. It was just too easy to grab drinks since it was a stone's throw from our condo.

Heather and I had been dancing to pop songs and singing together. I loved the feeling of getting lost in the music and moving my body to the beat, dancing with strangers while no one cared who you were and how wild you swayed.

I was excited to think Heather and I could become friends. I mean, we had just rocked out together, screaming the latest hit arm and arm. In my book, that was BFF status. Even if it was liquor induced, I was excited to get to know her and make a new friend. That was why I'd moved to the city in the first place. To live. To meet new people. To make friends. I hadn't lived here long, and it seemed like everyone already had their friend group locked down.

The social scene seemed like an impossibly hard thing to break into in your late twenties. I mean, I couldn't just send a note to someone that said, "Do you want to be my friend? Check 'yes' or 'no,'" which I had definitely done in elementary school. Someone had checked no. Kids were assholes. I don't even remember the girl's name, but I'd never forget how alone and rejected I felt when I saw that "no" had been decidedly checked.

To be fair, I knew I was a strange kid; that was why I tried so hard to … well, everything. The other kids knew I wasn't though. It's like a species thing, right? We have a sense of other. We can tell when one person in the group isn't like the rest of the herd. It upsets the balance, and people tend to not be up for the disturbance. I had always been the odd one out. It's not like I didn't try to fit in. But while most girls in my classes made straight A's, I had an ostracizing C average. They made fun of me for it. I knew I was smart; I could tell my mom exactly what we were studying as if I was teaching a class myself, but when it came to test taking or reading aloud, my mind would blank out. I was more interested in losing myself in stories, painting the day away, or following my mom everywhere while talking her ear off. And although I loved Barbie and dolls much like the other kids, I was more intrigued by Wednesday Addams and Elvira or Sailor Moon and Sabrina the Teenage Witch.

"Clarke? … Clarke! What you drinking tonight?" Morgan the bartender asked, breaking through my racing thoughts.

"Oh, sorry, Morgan!" I shook my head a bit to clear the fog. "A rum and coke and a tequila sunrise please."

"Coming right up."

When he'd returned, I'd thrown down two twenty-dollar bills on the bar to cover our tab and tip, grabbed the drinks, and headed back to the dance floor and to Heather, my shy little bird of a roommate who was smiling and laughing as the next pop song bounced through the crowd. That night had been such a good night.

And now Heather was dead. I could repeat it over and over, and it still didn't feel real. When EMTs arrived, they'd taken me outside and wrapped me in a foil blanket. Apparently, I'd been pale and clammy and breathing in shallow gasps. As I sat on the back bumper of an ambulance with my silver space blanket draped around my shoulders staring at our condo building, I couldn't wrap my head around the reality of it.

Our neighbors had come outside to see why all the cop cars and emergency service vehicles were there. The crime scene unit was inside doing their thing. They hadn't brought Heather out yet. I didn't think I wanted that image burned into my brain. Seeing half her arm hanging off her bed and her blood on the floor was enough for a lifetime of nightmare fuel.

I was vaguely aware of an officer speaking to me, but it sounded how Charlie Brown's teacher always sounded in the cartoon—*wah mah woh wah*. I could only make out every few words, and a weird high-pitched sound was drowning out everything. I knew I was still in shock; my teeth were chattering even though the evening air was mild. I'm pretty sure the officer was trying to figure out if I had a place to stay for a few days. All my stuff was inside though, and I didn't think I could gather the courage to go in and get it. I'm sure Alison would let me stay with her if I needed to.

Cops started running caution tape around the exterior of our building. I could hear the officers talking. One of them went up to a man who looked to be in charge and said, "Sir, we found no sign of forced entry. Nothing seems to be missing or disturbed, but we would have to let the roommate inside to confirm that for us. We found some footprints leading out the back entrance. The crime scene unit is identifying the type of shoes and size right now and is cross-referencing all the shoes inside the apartment to rule out any internal foul play."

Internal foul play? What the hell? That phrase sort of woke me out of my daze. They were treating this as a homicide. Something must have indicated that Heather didn't kill herself. I was stuck between being mildly relieved that she didn't hurt herself and terrified that a killer had entered our home.

No forced entry? The front door had been locked when I came home. I unlocked it to come in, I thought. Didn't I? Did Heather leave the back door unlocked? She wasn't usually that careless. She was a bit of a worrier and a bit skittish. I really didn't think that was something she'd forget.

I was racking my brain over and over. We always locked our doors. I mean, we lived in a nice enough area, but we were two females living alone. We weren't stupid, and after a homeless man had found his way into our community space stairwell one night and scared the hell out of some girl taking her trash down to the trash room, we were reminded to keep our guards up and doors locked. The homeless guy was harmless, but the next person to find their way inside the complex might not be. Well, shit, obviously not because Heather was fucking dead. No, not just dead—murdered!

Glancing down at my ruined pants coated in her blood, a flash of Heather's pale hand dangling off her bed went through my head. I shuddered. The sweatpants were stiffening in the places where the blood had dried.

I heard some commotion and shouts to clear the area. The coroner and his team walked out of the apartment carrying a large black zipped-up bag.

Fuck, it's a body bag, I thought. They were bringing Heather out. I didn't want to see it, but my eyes stayed glued to the lifeless figure being carried out.

Vomit rose in my throat. I gagged, jumped up, and threw up in the nearest bush.

CHAPTER 3

After emptying the entire contents of my stomach, I collapsed onto the nearest curb and wiped my mouth with the back of my sleeve. This outfit was toast anyway—as soon as I got access to my clothes inside, I'd be tossing or burning it.

A female officer walked toward me. She had a soft, curvy body and an even softer smile. Her curly hair was cropped short, and her impeccable makeup highlighted her dark complexion perfectly.

"Miss Carpenter? … Clarke Carpenter?"

"Yes," I croaked out, sounding like an eighty-year-old man with emphysema. The officer winced when she heard me.

"Miss Carpenter, we need you to come with us to the station. We need to ask you a few questions."

My stomach dropped like I'd swallowed a bowling ball. "What? Why?"

"It's just standard procedure, Miss Carpenter." She smiled reassuringly.

I barely registered that she had already helped me to my feet and guided me to one of the many cop cars that now lined our street. She opened the door to the backseat and gestured for me to get in. I sat behind the caged partition. The seat was cold and hard, and the car smelled musty.

Criminals sat back here, right? I didn't like how that made me feel.

I looked out the window and saw one of the crime scene investigators showing something to a few of the cops standing around the entrance to our condo. One motioned toward me. I couldn't make out anything they said, but unease settled in my belly like a fifty-pound weight as I took in the looks on their faces.

The ride to the police station barely took five minutes. Someone quickly escorted me inside and into a room with Interrogation Room A on the door. I'd seen these types of rooms in movies and crime shows. And here I was, about to sit at one of those cold metal tables. It was surreal. There was even a metal loop in the middle where they could attach handcuffs.

The stench coming off my shirt filled my nostrils, rolling my stomach. The sour smell of vomit and the rusty smell of dried blood permeated the empty room.

A chill went through my whole body. I had that same feeling I always had when I passed a cop on the highway. Even if I was doing the speed limit, I immediately felt like I was doing something illegal. Maybe I feared having my freedom taken away, feared a cage, or simply hated being in trouble. I usually did everything I could to stay under the radar and keep my head down so they wouldn't notice me.

The door opened, and a heavy-set man in his late fifties, maybe early sixties, walked in. He had a gray mustache that had yellowed at the edges, likely from years of smoking. His salt-and-pepper hair was combed over, poorly hiding his receding hairline. The lines between his brows pinched together as he took in my disheveled appearance with disgust. He pulled back the chair opposite me and sat down. He smelled like tobacco and vinegar, making my stomach turn yet again. I turned my head to hide my dry heave.

He placed a recorder in between us and turned it on.

"Miss Carpenter, I would like to ask you some questions," he started.

"Oh, sure, of course," I replied, trying to sound as normal as possible.

"What was the nature of your relationship with Heather Dunn?"

"Heather was my roommate, sir."

"Did you get along?" He prodded.

"Yes, we did. She was a great roommate. She always paid rent on time, kept to herself, was kind, cleaned up after herself …" I trailed off.

"How long had you known the deceased?"

"About a year. Yeah, she moved into my condo about a year ago."

"Can you think of a reason anyone would want to cause her harm? She have any enemies?"

"No, not at all. Not that I know of. I don't understand how this happened. I don't understand—"

"Where were you last night?" he continued.

"I was home. Why?"

"We found some disturbing evidence in your condo, Miss Carpenter," he said as he looked at me with disdain.

He shoved a photo of a soiled red shoe in front of me and asked accusingly, "Clarke, do you recognize this shoe?"

The shoe reminded me of a pair that Alison had bought me for my thirtieth birthday. They were gorgeous, red patent leather that sparkled, with four-inch heels, red leather souls, and likely had cost her more than my monthly mortgage. I wore them one time and promptly put them back into the box they came in to protect them.

"Um, it kind of looks like a pair I have. Why?"

"When we were processing the apartment, we found shoe prints leaving out the back door. Crime scene went through all the shoes in the house and found these shoved toward the back of your closet. They appear to match the shoe prints we found leading away from the crime scene, and they have trace amounts of blood on them. The DNA has confirmed it is Heather's blood."

"What ...?"

My mind was foggy, processing things slower than normal. As he continued to speak, each word started to hit home. Everything he'd said slowly clicked in place. This is an interrogation, I thought. I'm being interrogated. Do they think I did this? Wait, what the fuck is happening?

I started breathing rapidly, and my heart was racing. I felt nauseous again. An acidic taste filled my mouth. Don't throw up, I thought. Calm down, Clarke. Please don't throw up.

I was only catching every couple of words as the room got smaller. I gripped the table as my hands started shaking and my vision turned black around the edges.

"Sir?" I heard a female voice say. "Sir!" It was the same female officer from the crime scene. Officer Cain? Is that what her name badge said? She touched the man's shoulder. "Sir, I think she's having a panic attack. We should—"

"Miss Carpenter, are you with me?" The male officer pressed. "Do you understand what I'm saying to you?

Before we walk out of this room, I need you to understand that right now, the only evidence we have is implicating you as our number one suspect. The evidence tells a story, and right now, the story is pointing us toward you."

"But, no, you don't understand. I didn't—I'm not a—" my retort caught in my throat. "I was at work all day. I didn't do this."

"You said you were home last night."

"Yes, but—"

"Were you home between the hours of two and four a.m. last night, Miss Carpenter?"

"Yes, yes, I was home, but—"

"The crime scene unit estimated Heather Dunn's death to have occurred somewhere between those times. Our forensic pathologist will need to confirm that timeline, but right now, you were the only one on the premises when the crime was committed. By your own admission, you do not have an alibi. Your footprints with Miss Dunn's blood on them were found leaving the scene. As of now, you are being held on suspicion of murder in the first degree. I need you to understand this, Miss Carpenter."

Oh … my … God, I thought. I was home when Heather was murdered. I was passed out after three glasses of wine, having a sex dream when she took her last breaths. As someone came into our apartment and killed her. How was this possible? I had heard nothing.

My breathing had become painful. Get it together, Clarke, I thought. Breathe in slowly, breathe out slowly, breathe in slowly, breathe out slowly, big deep breath, and blow it out.

Then he started reading me the Miranda rights, the fucking Miranda rights.

"Clarke Carpenter, we are arresting you on suspicion of murder in the first degree of Heather Dunn …."

Officer Cain walked over, holding legit handcuffs. Her warm smile was a stark contrast to the situation we were in, but it made me feel comforted and safe somehow. Her dark-brown eyes softened as she walked over to me with the cuffs. She looked like she didn't want to be doing this. Weird. I mean, it's her job, right, but she seemed to feel sorry for me. Maybe she didn't think I could've murdered my roommate, but the male officer was looking at me like the scum of the earth. So much for the accused being innocent until proven guilty.

Her hands were soft as she gently clasped the first ring of the handcuffs onto my left hand, then the right, and tightened them. And man, no one tells you how uncomfortable those fuckers are. The cold metal bit my skin.

"Do you have a lawyer, Miss Carpenter?"

I couldn't answer her. I felt like I'd swallowed a bunch of cotton balls, and they were stuck in my throat.

Taking my silence as an answer, Officer Cain continued, "We can contact them for you, or the state will provide one for you. For now, I need to escort you down the hall to get changed and then to one of the holding cells."

"A phone call," I managed to say. When was my voice going to stop sounding like someone had crushed my vocal cords?

"What?" the male officer asked.

"I get a phone call, right?"

"Yes, ma'am. After we get you processed, we will come and get you to make your call," Officer Cain answered.

All I could think of was how I needed to get in touch with Alison, whose dad was a big-time criminal defense lawyer. I'd never met him before and certainly never thought I'd be reaching out to him for the first time in a professional sense.

Officer Cain led me down a corridor void of color. Everything was metal and shades of gray-monotone, like life didn't exist there. We stopped and went into a small room where a lone table held a folded khaki jumpsuit. Khaki: the bane of my existence. I'd graduated from a private school; it had been a never-ending sea of khaki. I'd sworn never to wear that color again, and here I was, on my way to a holding cell about to be head to toe in fucking khaki.

"Get changed and leave all your belongings and clothes on the table there," Officer Cain directed.

I got changed into the jumpsuit, the worst fabric I've ever worn, and was only slightly relieved to get out of my crusty blood-stained sweatpants and T-shirt. My feet were still bare from where I'd discarded my shoes when I got home from work. They were slightly blood stained, but most of it had flaked off as the blood dried.

When I finished getting dressed, Officer Cain opened the door and handed me some white slip-on tennis shoes to put on. She led me out into the hallway and down a series of other hallways through a labyrinth of gray. She halted at an empty cell, unlocked it, and motioned for me to go in.

I sat on a metal cot with a sad excuse for a mattress, a threadbare blanket, and the flattest pillow I'd ever seen. Even though the bedding looked stained, it didn't smell bad, and I was so tired. A wave of exhaustion hit me, and I lay down and closed my eyes. Questions raced through my mind: How did I get here? Who killed Heather? Why? I quickly drifted off, surrendering to the bone-tiredness that I felt.

Driving across a land-bridge, I barreled toward a raging storm. I knew I had to reach the other side; I couldn't go back, only forward, like I was on a self-propelled ride. Terror enveloped me as I took note of how close the water was getting to my car and how quickly the water level was surging.

I screamed as the waves reached skyscraper heights. Though the water was rising and the storm raging, the view was clear, as if my imminent doom needed to be viewed without obstruction. I continued driving until I was compelled to turn my head to my right; at the same time, the crest of a skyscraper-sized wave descended onto my car; I knew it was the end, and there was no avoiding it; I closed my eyes and surrendered ....

I blinked my eyes open wide. I was safe. I was whole, still cocooned in my blankets in bed. Safe in my condo in the city. I shook off the dream as I'd done so many times before. "It's just a dream," I said to the empty room.

It was always just a dream, but they always felt like ... more. I'd lose myself every night, only to claw my way back to reality. I'd wake up each morning relieved that, somehow, I'd made it back. I'd relish knowing that it was only a dream and none of it was real.

Stretching, I crawled my way out of my warm bed, ready to greet the day. I headed to the bathroom, mindlessly moving through my morning routine. As I walked out into the hallway, I slipped in something wet. My feet flew out from under me, and I fell—hard. Now drenched in whatever I'd slipped in, my arm was coated in a sticky warm red liquid that was blood red. Heather ... Heather's blood ...

"Miss! Miss! Wake up!"

"Hey, bitch, keep it down!"

I woke up to people yelling at me from their own cells up and down the corridor. I'd screamed in my sleep. I was still in the gray prison on a hard cot, locked in a cell. Yeah, this is reality, I thought; this is where I really am. How long had I been out? Wasn't someone supposed to come get me for my phone call?

I hadn't had that dream in a while, the one where I'm pretty sure I drown at the end but always wake up before that happens. I'd almost drowned when I was a kid, but a powerful undercurrent had pulled me to the shoreline, miraculously saving me. You'd think that my current trauma started the storm dream, but nope, the dream came long before.

I've had recurring and vividly real dreams for as long as I can remember. I used to be afraid to go to sleep because the world awaiting me was sometimes so real and terrifying. Either the imagery or energy was filled with dread.

Maybe I was having the dream again because I felt like I was drowning in the waking world. I couldn't seem to get a footing anywhere, and my body felt like lead.

As I sat on my cot trying to get the dream out of my head, a deep-rooted sadness washed over me and dragged me under. I sank deeper and deeper until something like a phantom tentacle reached out from the icy depths and wrapped around me, cutting off my breath and circulation. I couldn't breathe or move or see a way out. The cold seeped into my bones, chilling me from the inside out as I lost my sense of direction.

I remained frozen like that for who knows how long. I felt like time was speeding by, leaving me in its wake, and simultaneously rowing by casually, laughing at me in my stasis. I'd have given anything at that moment for some sort of reprieve, but it never came. I feared that even when this moment passed, something would be irrevocably changed in me. A chunk would be missing from the very thing that made me who I was, something I didn't think I'd ever get back.

Had it really just been this morning that I'd woken up dreaming about sex? Only a few measly hours since everything had changed? I felt hopeless and forlorn: magic didn't exist; there weren't endless possibilities; that fucking cat with the crescent moon scar never showed up; and that long-lost family member never called to tell me I was a long-lost princess. Seriously, fuck that family member and that cat, and fuck Lucy and her adventures. Fuck them all. I had been so determined to start my new life with endless possibilities, believing something bigger was waiting out there for me. Well, my ass was in a box, a cold box with bars, and nothing bigger was waiting for me. Not anymore.

CHAPTER 4

"Lights out!" someone yelled.

"Hey!" I yelled back, "What about my phone call?"

No response. "Well, fuck! Are they really going to turn out all the lights?" I said aloud to my cell bars, which also didn't respond. What was worse than cold bars and a depressing sea of gray? Pitch-black darkness, that's what. When the lights went out, the windowless jail became a sea of black.

My heart stuttered as darkness filled the air. The atmosphere of the room changed, as if I was in a spaceship and something had breached the hull and sucked all the air out. My ears rang. Why was it that in the dark, your senses heightened, and you could hear everything and nothing at all? My mind was conjuring footsteps and voices as I sat alone, shivering with fear.

I waited for my eyes to adjust, but even minutes later I couldn't see my hand in front of my face. My mind wandered to another dark room. I breathed in a deep sigh as I thought of Heather. My quiet, sweet, meek roommate had been killed. I wished I had known more about her. I wished we would've gotten closer. We'd gone out once together and had a blast, but she'd seemed to pull back from me after that. She was estranged from her family, but I didn't know why. Would anyone other than me care she was dead? Would there be a funeral? Who would be there?

Heather had become even more withdrawn after I'd met my best friend, Alison, at a concert, one I'd begged Heather to come to with me. Alison's personality had likely intimidated her. Heather and Alison were opposites. Alison was a wrecking ball. She came into my life determined to love me, inserted herself into every corner of my world, and drew me into hers. Our lives quickly intertwined. Her friendship came with a built-in community, a group of friends I didn't have to break into. We had little in common except our love for red wine and romantic comedies, but she reminded me so much of my mom with her vivacious, infectious personality. She was the yang to my yin, pushing me out of my comfort zone and helping build back the confidence that seemed to evaporate with my mother's ghost. She became the cheerleader in my life that made me nostalgic for those dark days of my childhood when my mom would constantly champion me and lift me up. Alison, without knowing it, brought back a little bit of what I'd been missing without my mom. No one would ever take Mom's place in my heart, but the achy, empty void I'd felt for years wasn't so acute with Alison in my life.

Heather, in contrast, was walled off and detached. She wasn't unkind at all, just an introvert who loved her solitude. I knew little to nothing about her. She didn't seem to have friends, and she was more than content to have me as a companionable roommate than an actual friend. Her death seemed even more mysterious to me because of how little we knew each other.

The darkness started playing tricks on me with no difference between eyes opened or eyes closed. My mind created endlessly shifting shapes in the void. Sometimes they would resolve into a lifeless arm hanging over a bed and dissolve into sweeping waves. I felt like I was losing touch with reality as my dreams weaved into my waking state. I wondered how long I'd been there. A few hours? A few days? Time seemed irrelevant.

Floating in an ocean of despair, I breathed in a familiar scent that smelled faintly of a skunk that had rolled around in pine needles. The air had become a fog rolling through the sea of endless night. My nostrils constricted as I took the fog into my lungs. I knew it was impossible, but as I inhaled the unmistakable smell of marijuana, I felt calm, subdued, and weightless. My shoulders slumped, my muscles relaxed, and my body blissfully numbed.

While my mind had become a twisted mess of blurred reality and fiction, of dreaming and waking, at this moment I no longer cared.

From the corner of my left eye, light broke through my trance, and I saw a tiny reddish-black light, like a little blinking siren. It seemed to move closer to where I lay on my sad cot, like an angry firefly dancing toward me. I heard someone take a deep inhale and felt a cloud of smoke blow into my face. I started coughing. Blinking through the plume of smoke, I looked up at a barely lit face. Terrified that I might not be alone in here, I attempted to force my mind to be more alert and lucid.

He looked ominous because I could only see what the cherry on his joint illuminated, like how you look when you hold a flashlight under your face while you're telling spooky stories around a campfire. His eyes glowed with mischief, but that wasn't all I could see. The joint also outlined the tip of his nose and the contours of his mouth.

I closed my eyes and shook my head in disbelief and was shocked to see he was still there—and was now grinning at me. It reminded me of the smile of the Cheshire Cat from one of my favorite books, Alice in Wonderland. I always loved reading about Alice falling down a rabbit hole into a world of wonder and fantasy.

I decided maybe I should say hello to this new person in the room.

"Hello?"

Silence.

"Hello?" I called out again, a little louder.

"You can see me? That's ... surprising," a male voice answered me, laced with shock.

"I agree since I'm sure this is one of the weirder dreams my subconscious has conjured. I'm also surprised to be seeing you."

He stared at me, and I stared back.

His unwavering attention unnerved me.

"Are you real?" I asked.

"That's an interesting question. Are *you* real?" he answered.

"Good diversion tactic. And I will answer your question even though you haven't answered mine." I said pointedly. "I don't know what is real now. I mean, when I'm awake and lucid, my perception is that I am real. Right now, we are stuck somewhere in my mind while—I hope—I'm getting some much-needed rest."

"I'm curious. Why would you think I am not real?"

"Besides the fact that most of my dreams are as vivid as you are currently?" I took his silence as a cue to keep on talking. "First of all, you seem to be a male in what I can only assume is the female side of the holding cells in this place. And, secondly, you seem to be smoking a joint, and that's obviously impossible because we are in jail."

"I see. Your reasoning is very astute."

"Thank you. I think. Well, while I've appreciated this interaction, I think I'd like to stop talking to myself and enjoy some peace and quiet."

I decided sitting by the creepy toilet in the opposite corner would be better than continuing to indulge this delusion. I got off my bed and shuffled to the far side of the room until my shins hit the toilet's side. I turned and sat, leaning against the cold metal toilet and hugged my knees to my chest. Horribly uncomfortable and honestly shocked not to hear a reply from the man my mind had conjured, I drifted off.

CHAPTER 5

Darkness surrounded me in a humid and suffocating place. A sticky red mist hung in the air; it clung to my skin, leaving it damp. Shafts of light peaked through the misty shadows. The places where they reached my skin seemed to smoke. I need to leave, I thought to myself; I need to get out of here.

"Clarke," a voice beckoned through the void. A hand reached through the darkness, and as I backed away from its grasp, I fell backward into a swamp-like bog. It was deeper than it appeared. Desperate, I clawed my way back to the surface, choking up the dank and murky water, and began screaming.

I awoke with a jerk. I reached for my throat, which felt hot and tight as if I'd been screaming. Perhaps it was still raw from screaming when I found Heather.

What had I been dreaming? Was I having a nightmare? My heart rate suggested that I had been, but I'd forgotten what it was about as soon as I'd woken up. I hated that—wanting to remember something just barely out of reach but coming up blank—especially since not remembering it didn't make the weird feeling any easier to shake off. I rubbed my hands up and down my arms to ease my frayed nerves, but the pinch of pain I felt stopped me.

"What the—" I said as I looked down at my hands and forearms. My skin was blotchy and red with welts forming in some places. "Am I having an allergic reaction?" I asked. The bed was probably infested with god knew what, and the jumpsuit they gave me was honestly the most uncomfortable, itchy fabric. "Great, I'm breaking out in hives. Maybe I'll go into anaphylaxis and die; then I'll get out of here." A dark, sardonic laugh came from my belly, which was frightening even to me. Geez, I'd gone to a dark place quickly.

A door down the hall banged open, and the heavy footsteps of a man in boots approached. I jumped up quickly and stood at attention, readying myself for whatever was coming my way.

"Cell 9, Clarke Carpenter?" A male officer I had not yet met addressed me.

"Yes, that's me."

"Stand over by the back wall, hands above your head."

He unlocked the door, came toward me, cuffed me, attached a heavy chain to them, and walked me out into the hallway. The officer was short and stout, standing about my height with a stern face peppered with pock marks—the sign of childhood acne—and deep-set forehead lines. His hair was sheared bald, resembling a shiny pale bowling ball. His eyes held no kindness as he continued speaking to me.

"You got one phone call. I hope you have some numbers memorized, or you'll be shit out of luck. You get five minutes, and I will stand here the whole time. If you're in here, you've lost your right to privacy, so don't get any ideas," he said in a clipped tone. Gesturing to his wristwatch, he continued. "Keep it short and sweet, and we won't have no problems."

Oh, this guy was chipper. Thankfully, I had Alison's number memorized. Like, who the hell knows numbers anymore? That's what cell phones are for, right?

He led me down the hall and opened a door into a large room that was lined with phones on one wall. Picking up the receiver, so thankful the phone smelled of fresh disinfectant, I dialed Alison's number.

"This is the Charlotte-Mecklenburg Police Department with a collect call from Clarke Carpenter. Will you accept the charges?"

"Oh, fuck! Yes! Shit! I mean, yes, yeah." I heard Alison fumble her reply.

"Alison—"

"Holy shit, Clarke! Girl, you sound terrible! I've been freaking out! Are you okay? I came to the police station, but they wouldn't let me see you. I called my dad, and he said someone from his firm would try to get you out. What do you need? What can I do? I can't believe Heather is dead. How could they think you were capable of hurting her?!"

"Alison, wow, hold on. I only get a few minutes here. Tell your dad I said thank you, and I do need legal representation, so I would love to take him up on his offer. What I need to know is—and I really hate to ask this—but can you find out if they have set bail yet? I don't want to spend another night in this place if I can help it. If they have, can you pay it for me? I wouldn't ask if—"

"Girl"—Alison popped her gum, which she always seemed to be chewing—"I already found that out when I came to the station. Me and the crew pooled our money together, and I'm coming up there to pay it today."

"Oh my god, Alison, thank you! You guys are amazing." My voice cracked with emotion. "I'll pay you back. I swear. How much was it? I should have enough in my savings to pay you back when I get out." I was so glad they had set a bail. I needed to get out of here before I genuinely lost my mind.

"First of all, chill on the paying us back thing. It's the last thing you need to worry about. We love you. Of course, we would be there for you."

"One minute," the officer interrupted rudely.

"Okay, Clarke, real quick, when I called the station this morning, they told me that even if I paid your bail, you'd need to be committed to a willing party for temporary housing, or you'll have to be in some safe house with an officer. Gross! So I had Daddy pull some strings so I could take you in because you'll be under house arrest, and you can't go back to your place yet because it's still an active crime scene. Isn't that great! I figured you'd love it, and I knew you wouldn't want to stay with anyone else, and since your parents live so far away, you probably couldn't go there. So we are gonna be roomies, babe!"

A pang of guilt struck me. I had never told my friends here that I was basically an orphan. After my mom's passing, my dad had passed away from a massive heart attack. My mom's death had left a giant hole in my heart. Dad took it harder than I thought he would, and his health declined quickly. The doctors said he'd been drinking a lot, which escalated an underlying condition. He and I were never close, but he'd been the only person I had left, and I loved him. It was a bit of a tragic moment in my life that I liked to keep to myself, which is why everyone thought my parents were back in my hometown, living their best lives. I didn't want pity and hated rehashing the story; I simply didn't want to talk about it.

I patted the space on my chest where the necklace my mom gave me right before she died normally hung. I felt naked and sad that it was so far away from me now. She'd charged me with keeping it safe and cherished: "Keep this close and think of me. I will never be far from you, my girl." A small tear escaped my eye, and I quickly wiped it away. Taking a reinforcing breath, I answered Alison.

"Holy shit, Alison, thank you so much. I don't even know—"

"Girl, my dad told me you're in deep shit. Something about bloody shoe prints, a missing murder weapon, and—girl, did you know they think Heather was stabbed? *Stabbed,* girl! I mean, what a way to—"

Click.

"Your five minutes is up," the officer interrupted.

No way in fuck that was five minutes, I thought as red rage ran through my body. What a dick! It took everything I had not to mouth off to him, but I quickly schooled my features to appear unbothered. Breathe in slowly, breathe out slowly, Clarke. Breathe in slowly, breathe out slowly. Big deep breath and let it out. Calm. I didn't need to do anything to jeopardize getting out of here.

He walked me back to my cell wordlessly. Thankful for that small mercy, I plopped down on my cot. The cell door slammed shut with a loud, abrasive clang. But for the first time since I was arrested, I felt a tiny spark of hope. My friends had come through for me.

Being a loner most of my life, I was still surprised when people wanted to love me and be there for me. My mom and I had always been tight, but my friendships were a different story. I'd felt like everyone else had an ulterior motive, or at the most unexpected moment, they'd flip on me and turn into a different person. This was something that had happened to me repeatedly with anyone I had gotten close to. The last friend I'd let in, well, let's just say it ended badly.

I even had a playlist on my phone called "I hate best friends." I know, I know—who hates best friends, right? Well, I did for a long time with good reason.

Take Amber for example. Amber and I had been inseparable since the fourth grade when we bonded over our matching Lisa Frank lunch boxes. She wanted to spend the night at my house every weekend. I think my parents obliged because I'd really not had any close friends before, and I think they were secretly relieved. Finally, their weird outcast of a daughter had a friend. After elementary school, we never attended the same school but remained friends despite the distance.

Amber liked to paint and draw like me, and she loved watching anime shows. It was so nice having a friend who wanted to spend so much time with me doing things I already enjoyed doing. I was so thankful to finally have a best friend that I think I blocked out all the red flags.

Truthfully, it wasn't all sunshine and rainbows; we had our quarrels over the years, and looking back, I shouldn't have been so shocked when things went sideways. Instead, it completely blindsided me. It happened right after I started dating my first actual boyfriend, Julian. I met him when we were both freshmen at the community college near my parents' house. I really liked him and fell in love with him almost immediately. We spent all our free time together.

Amber and I had made plans to live together while I went to community college and she started at the state school nearby, but after I met Julian, he convinced me to move into his apartment instead. I knew the girl code said I should've stayed with the original plan, but I was young and in love and thought I was doing the right thing.

One night, my boyfriend and I were hanging out at our apartment, and I felt a prickle of awareness at the nape of my neck. You know, that feeling when you are being watched. I turned to look out the glass sliding doors of our apartment balcony. Staring daggers back at me was my best friend, Amber. It had been raining, so she looked like some kind of creepy apparition. The balcony off the apartment was on the second story of our building. I didn't know how the hell she climbed up. Was she secretly a parkour expert or something? She was standing there staring at me with angry, mascara-laden tears mixed with rain streaming down her face, so I got up to open the door.

She was holding a box of now-ruined photos of us, and when I asked her what the hell was going on, she said she felt like she was losing me and started yelling at me for not answering my door. I tried explaining that I hadn't even heard her knock—not even mentioning why the hell she'd climbed to the second story instead of texting me to let her into our building—but she wasn't having it. She continued her yelling while delving into how she really felt about me breaking our living plans. Apparently, she'd held a lot back during our previous conversation on the matter.

My boyfriend picked that moment to step out to see what was going on. "It's all your fault," she started screaming at him. She blamed him for the growing distance between her and me, and accused him of replacing her and ruining our plans. She said I'd changed and that she missed me, missed us. I was struck silent. Damn straight, I'd changed. I was happy for the first time in my life. Couldn't she understand that? I wasn't alone, and for the first time, I felt beautiful and cherished by someone other than my mom. It was an intoxicating feeling. I think I said something like, why couldn't she just be happy for me, and why was me being happy and having a boyfriend such a problem for her? Obviously, it was the wrong thing to say. She then turned toward my boyfriend, voice dripping with disgust and ire: "I'll kill you if you don't move!" she screamed. He'd moved into a defensive position between her and me.

So quickly that I didn't see it coming, she grasped the shoebox full of photos, swung it in an arc as hard as she could, and slammed my boyfriend in the temple. He stumbled backward and slipped on the rain-drenched wood of the balcony while grasping at the closest thing to keep him upright. Unfortunately, it was Amber. She slipped too, and to my complete horror, they slammed into the balcony railing. It dislodged, and they both fell over the edge.

I think I started screaming, their lives flashing before my eyes. My best friend and boyfriend were going to die or, at the very least, be seriously injured. My heart and lungs froze.

Suddenly, a powerful gust of wind broke against the building, cushioning their landing and miraculously saving their lives. I'd been certain they were going to die. My hand went to rest over my wildly thumping heart.

Still, I'd heard a sickening crack, a cringe-worthy pop, and some groans. I turned and ran through the apartment, threw open our door, and ran down two flights of steps and out the front entrance.

Amber and Julian lay on the ground—her clutching her ankle while he was clutching his arm. I dialed 911, and shortly afterward, emergency services arrived at our apartment building.

Amber said that Julian pushed her. Julian said Amber pushed him. They were both pissed at me. The police took my statement and took Amber in for questioning. I later found out that they had committed her to a psychiatric hospital.

Julian decided I was more trouble than I was worth and promptly broke up with me. He had been trying to get a football scout to pick him up so he could get a scholarship to the state school Amber attended, and he blamed me for his injured arm and ruined future.

Shortly after that, I received a disturbing voicemail from Amber telling me it was all my fault and that she'd tried to commit suicide twice. She said she would never forgive me for my statement that aided in her commitment. I became very guarded for a long time after that, keeping friends and potential boyfriends at arm's length.

I now understand some things that I was too immature and naïve to see back then. Amber's anger at me was warranted, but her actions that night were uncalled for.

Julian blaming me for Amber's actions was also valid. I'd broken a promise to her. However, his decision to walk away with no accountability was wrong. He had started the entire chain of events by convincing me to move in with him instead of Amber; he knew about my plans with Amber and had lobbied hard for me to change my mind. Of course, moving in with him was ultimately my decision.

All relationships are complicated, no matter if it is a friend, lover, or relative. So taking a page from Julian's book, I'd decided that they're all more trouble than they're worth and would rely solely on myself.

After my parents' deaths though, I'd missed the camaraderie of friendship, the touch of someone who loves me, and the warm feeling you get only from a mother's hug. Moving to Charlotte, I'd put myself out there again.

After Amber, I really hadn't opened up to anyone else until I met Alison. She kind of bulldozed through that layer of ice around my heart and didn't let me push her away. It was comforting really, having someone who loved me that much, someone to push past my comfort zone and declare themselves my best friend.

Alison had proved to me time and time again that she was there for the long haul. Even though she didn't know about my mom's death, she could always tell when my mood soured, and she would always do something to cheer me up. Her love language was gift giving, and anytime she glimpsed past the walls I'd built to hide my emotions, she'd see when I was down and bring me my favorite snacks or buy me something new to wear. The little things always meant the most to me though, and she was there for me when it counted. Like there were times when I felt insecure about being a thirty-year-old college student with a bunch of eighteen- to twenty-one-year-olds, but she would tell me that sort of thinking was old-fashioned and encourage me that it was never too late to get a degree. She bragged about me in front of our friends, saying that I was her smartest friend and that she couldn't wait to call me Professor Carpenter. I would explain to her that I was getting my bachelor's degree and wouldn't be a professor, but she would shush me and laugh. I loved the way she could make me feel like my insecurities were all in my head, that there was no way I couldn't see how amazing I was, or how proud I should be that I was working a full-time job and going back to school.

I was so thankful for her. She was my best friend now, even if I'd sworn to never have one again.

CHAPTER 6

Alison had crashed into my life six months ago. I'd begged Heather to come with me to see my favorite local band, but she said that she had to get up early and that the last time she'd gone out with me, she'd had to nap under her desk at her office job and hug a trash can all day. I'd felt a bit guilty for that, so I couldn't blame her for sitting this one out.

Swaying my hips to the music, I'd stopped caring that I was at the show alone. I was dragged out of my trance as a body knocked into mine, spilling half of my drink all over the floor.

"What the—"

"Oh my god!" the girl practically screamed in my ear. "I'm so sorry! Holy shit, girl, I'm so sorry! I'm Alison. What was in that? I'll go buy you another one. I'm so sorry. Shit, I'm such an asshole."

I looked at the girl in front of me who was having a verbal panic attack over spilling my drink. She was beautiful, gorgeous even, and I liked her immediately. She had long platinum-blonde hair that hung in beachy waves down her back, sparkling bright-blue eyes, and model-like features with perfect curves. She looked like Barbie come to life, complete with her all-pink outfit. She reminded me of the popular girl in school who everyone loved to hate but secretly wanted to date. She was smiling at me with a giant full-toothed smile—it was infectious.

"Oh, it's okay. It was just an accident. You don't need to."

"Nonsense," she said as she looped her arm through mine and leaned in. "You're coming with me to the bar."

I let Alison lead me out of the crowd and toward the bar in the next room.

She practically laid her body across the bar, her ample cleavage spilling dangerously out of her top, and yelled, "Hey, pretty boy, I need two shots of Jose and …" She looked at me, waiting for me to tell her what I was drinking.

"Oh, it was a tequila sunrise, but you don't have to."

"Who drinks that anymore, girl?" She turned back toward the bartender, "And a tequila sunrise for my friend here, and put it on my tab."

The bartender looked her way, winked, and started making our drinks.

Alison sank off the bar and looked at me, "Hey, girl, what's your name? I saw you dancing in there earlier; it didn't seem like you were with anyone. Are you here alone? You should hang with me—us. My whole crew is here. We are toward the front of the crowd in there."

Wow, she wasn't having a verbal panic attack earlier, I thought, this is just how she talks. Chuckling a little to myself, I answered, "I'm Clarke, and I'm not hanging with anyone tonight. I know it's super lame, but I couldn't get anyone to come with me, and this is one of my favorite bands."

"Nice to meet you, Clarke, and that's not lame at all. It shows you're a committed fan. I like that. I'm a big fan of all things music. All my friends are either in a band, were in a band, or want to be in a band." She laughed, big and loud, and turned to where the bartender called her name. She took the two tequila shots from him and shoved one in my hand.

"To new friends," she'd said as she plucked out the gum she'd been chewing, clinked her shot to mine, knocked it down on the bar, tilted her head back, and downed the tequila.

"To new friends," I repeated with a knot forming in my throat. Unexpected emotion welled up as I felt a feeling of being home, being safe. I felt like I'd just met not a stranger but someone I'd known for years. This girl in front of me was everything I had moved to the city to become: confident, outgoing, and unapologetically herself. I didn't think I was lucky enough to have found two kindred spirits in my lifetime, but the hope that Alison could be something close warmed my heart. Smiling at the prospect, I took the shot exactly how Alison—

"Carpenter!" The rude officer from earlier broke through my memory of the first time I'd met Alison.

"Yes, sir," I saluted sarcastically. That earned me a harsh glare. Whoops.

"Some sucker paid your bail. Thought you'd wanna know. It'll take a few more hours, but you'll be outta here soon."

"Amazing." I sighed with relief and slouched back onto my cot.

"I wouldn't get used to it though. I have a feeling we'll be seeing you around here real soon." He smirked cruelly.

Not if I can help it, I thought. I never wanted to see that place again as long as I lived. Alison's dad was a lawyer who owned his own firm, and she'd said they were already working on my case. Things had to be looking up, right? He seemed to be very wealthy if Alison's depictions were to be trusted. That led me to believe he had to be successful at what he did.

I yawned and did a little stretch. I had to have slept for half the time I'd been in there, but I was more exhausted than I'd ever been in my whole life. I guess it was emotional exhaustion, but the room itself seemed to siphon any energy I had. I'd eaten very little, which could have been a contributing factor too. I had a lot of food allergies, and the prison food was less than accommodating. The two meals they'd brought were chicken and lasagna. I was mostly vegan, so that didn't work for me. I didn't complain though. I don't think I could've eaten if they had brought me my favorite vegan popcorn. My stomach was in knots. Come to think of it, my whole body hurt, my bones were achy, and I had a splitting headache. I felt like I was getting sick, and I never got sick. I decided to give in to my exhaustion again. I might as well sleep through as much of this as I can, I thought and let my eyes drifted closed ….

I heard a fast, whooshing sound and felt the air rushing up around my body. I was falling fast. The air caught in my lungs as I tried desperately to take in a breath. I flailed my arms as if to catch myself on something or stop the momentum of my high-speed descent. My hand slammed down on a hard surface, and I jolted up.

Slamming my hand down on my cot, I realized I wasn't falling, just falling asleep. Idiot, I thought, how long was I out? I tried to lull myself back to sleep, but unfortunately, I was wide awake.

When I wasn't sleeping, my thoughts had been painfully full of visions of Heather. I had to come up with a plan to prove I didn't murder her and try to get the authorities to continue to investigate. I knew I didn't kill her, so who the hell did? They had to have found something at our apartment other than bloody footprints. What about fingerprints? A murder weapon? That's right—Alison said that it was missing.

Another officer I'd not met before came by when it was time for lights out to tell me that my processing was finished and that they would have me out by morning. The darkness continued to play tricks on me by summoning another bizarre conversation with my nameless, imaginary friend. It was slightly comforting to talk to someone, even if I knew it was basically me talking to myself. It helped pass the time until daybreak when they'd bring me shitty food I could barely eat and water that tasted like they mixed it with cleaning supplies. One more night. One more shitty, inedible meal.

Surrendering to my ten-pound eyelids, I curled up in the fetal position on my cot with the comfort of knowing this would be the last time I had to fall asleep in the gray void.

Fear prickled my body as an overwhelming sense of dread ran through my nervous system. I opened my eyes and took in the destruction around me.

Bedlam.

The terrain around me sizzled and smoked. I could see only ash all the way to the horizon. The remnants of a world once alive withered around me, broken and destroyed. My heart ached with a loss so deep that I was sure it was breaking.

What had happened here?

"Miss Carpenter," someone was calling my name softly and rocking my shoulder slightly. Dread and fear had paralyzed the lower half of my body, and I was terrified to open my eyes. Whatever I'd been dreaming left a foreboding signature in its wake.

"Clarke?" A kind voice beckoned me again through my veil of sleep.

I peeled one eye open, happy to see Officer Cain peering back at me. She offered me another kind smile as I pushed up to a seated position on the cot.

"I'm sorry to wake you, but it's morning," Officer Cain cooed warmly. "I'm here to take you to fill out some paperwork, fit you for your ankle monitor, and get you out of here."

Feeling relieved and excited—I was getting out—I smiled back at her. "I'm always up for getting some new jewelry. What about my clothes? Do I wear this lovely jumpsuit home?" I gestured to my prison outfit.

"No, ma'am, you don't take those with you. Unfortunately, you will not be getting the clothes you wore here back. At least not for a while. We have collected them for evidence."

Understanding dawned on me. "That makes sense," I replied. "Honestly, if I never have to see those clothes again, I'm good."

Officer Cain answered with an understanding smile. "Your friend is here to collect you, and she brought you some clean clothes and shoes to change into."

"Wow, Alison, coming in for the win again."

"Huh?"

"Oh, never mind, just thankful for good friends is all," I answered as she led me down the labyrinth of halls that I was weirdly getting accustomed to. She opened a door and led me to sit down in a metal chair. The cold of the chair seeped through my bones as I sat down. I was introduced to a girl about my age with dark brown hair cut perfectly into a sharp A-line bob with equally sharp eyebrow-dusting bangs, brownish eyes, and black-rimmed glasses. She looked like someone I'd be friends with, but also like a nerdy gamer geek dressed up as a police officer. Her name was Officer Luck, and she asked me to prop my foot up onto a stool in front of her. She fitted me for my ankle monitor and turned toward her computer, where she keyed in Alison's address and created a one-foot perimeter around her home. That's about all the leeway I would get, she explained.

Thanking Officer Luck, I exited the room with Officer Cain. She took me to the same small holding room where I'd received my jailhouse jumpsuit and directed me to the pile of clothes on the table. I also noted a large clear plastic bag full of my personal effects. I smiled as I saw the bee keychain peeking out through the bag. I'd bought it at an Uptown gift shop the first week I moved there. I took it as a sign that I'd made the right choice. I loved bees and what they represented to me—magical little creatures who flew despite the fact that it was scientifically impossible for them to do so.

"I also noticed the red breakouts on your arms. I know sometimes these jumpsuits aren't the most comfortable. So I grabbed some ointment from the first aid kit for you."

"Thank you so much," I said, taking the ointment from Officer Cain, touched by her kind gesture.

She smiled warmly and exited the room.

"Finally, soft clothes," I said to the empty room. "Maybe these rashes will go away." I quickly changed out of my jumpsuit, opened the small package of cream for the welts on my arms and hands, and applied the soothing balm. I pulled on the clothes Alison had brought for me. To say we were not the same size was an understatement. My boobs, hips, and ass were all on the plump side, while Alison was tall with a slender frame and perfect B-cup boobs. Her clothes made me look like I was in jail for something way more fun than murder—not that murder is fun! Well, I guess it is to a psychopath.

Lastly, I put on Alison's shoes. Luckily, we had the exact same shoe size. I opened the plastic bag and emptied the contents. My keys, wallet, and cell phone were all accounted for.

Feeling more like a human than I had in days, I followed Officer Cain to another room where I filled out form after form. Getting arrested came with lots of paperwork, apparently.

When I rounded the corner of the waiting area to leave, Alison spotted me right away and barreled into me with a force I didn't think her slight frame was capable of.

"Clarke, girl, oh my god, you look terrible," she said while somehow simultaneously smacking her gum. "Let's get the hell out of here. Whoa, your boobs look incredible in my shirt! Come on, I've got all your favorite foods at my place and some surprises," she said as she looped her arm through mine.

I smiled, my heart warming at the normality of Alison's verbal diarrhea. I loved that girl.

CHAPTER 7

Alison had settled me into her one-bedroom apartment in South End, the trendy district just south of Uptown Charlotte, where she'd made up the couch for me to sleep on. She'd had to continue with her normal work routine as a hair stylist at Cache, a popular salon Uptown, and apologized for having to leave me alone during the day. Honestly though, I'd welcomed the solitude. All I'd wanted to do was veg out and not think. I just wanted sleep, binge-watch trashy TV, and eat all the vegan treats Alison had stocked in the kitchen for me.

I admired Alison's drive to still keep a job despite the fact that her dad paid for her pricy rent. Our similarities ended with our work ethic though. While she had enjoyed a very cushy upbringing with loads of friends, I'd been the outcast with a modest home. Alison was generous with the abundance she'd been given, always picking up the tab before her friends could object and working with a local nonprofit to donate her time and talent giving homeless people free haircuts to help them look more presentable for job interviews.

After a few days of resting and being lazy, I felt restless. I needed to get out of there. I'd traded one prison for another—albeit a much more comfortable one. I felt trapped. Scratch that—I was trapped. I was suffocating, like fate was holding a giant pillow over my face.

A few weeks ago, I'd been a master of positivity, championing myself daily, not letting my thoughts turn dark. I'd turned a corner in my struggles with my previous life of battling anxiety and depression. And now … I just felt … powerless.

As a little girl, I'd craved power. Strength. Something that would give me an edge over all the bad things in my life. Although my home life had been less than perfect, I'd known it wasn't as bad as some other kids.

My mom was a saint. She loved me so fiercely and never made me feel how everyone else did outside of my house—small, weird, strange, or unseen. She was a beautiful woman with thick black wavy hair that fell around her shoulders and dark-brown eyes that sparkled with kindness. And she was so tall, way taller than my five-foot-three stature and almost taller than my dad.

My dad, he was another story. He was also tall by anyone's standards, with sturdy shoulders, strong and intimidating features, dark-brown eyes, and brownish-red hair cut to just below his ears. His personality was like Dr. Jekyll and Mr. Hyde. Well, Dr. Jekyll without the genius; I never took Dad for an overly intelligent man. For no reason at all (no reason that warranted the type of behavior in my eyes), he would turn into a scary, howling monster. Yelling, screaming, throwing things, breaking things, calling me names, calling my mom names—he'd become unhinged.

I always walked on eggshells. I learned to avoid his wrath by making myself small, not taking up space, and breathing so shallowly that I made no sound. I can't say that I feared him exactly. The desire to avoid invoking his explosive behavior was only partly self-preservation; mostly, I wanted to protect my mom from his wrath. He'd often take out his anger two-fold: first on me when I'd done something to set him off and then on my mom as if it was her fault that I was such a terrible, unruly child.

Someone who was supposed to love you wasn't supposed to treat you like that, right? He never physically hit me, and I never saw him hit my mom, but sometimes I wished he had. At least then one of us would have had an injury for someone to see, to put a stop to. No, the scars he inflicted were on the inside, hidden so no one really knew. Of course, as a kid, I was too embarrassed to tell anyone about it. He was a charmer to everyone else, so who would believe me? Keeping that secret was isolating. I often felt alone, even in a crowded room.

I never understood why my mom stayed with him for so long, but maybe she didn't have the strength to leave. Maybe staying was a twisted form of strength. I really didn't know. All I knew was that I needed to make it stop for me and for her. I wanted a shield, a power, a strength to be brave enough to fight back, to fight the bully at home and the bullies at school.

My first best friend, Virginia, had become the worst bully of them all. She and I had become best friends in preschool before anyone cared about being cool or even knew the meaning of the word. We had sleepovers and talked about how we'd be best friends forever and couldn't wait to attend kindergarten together. I'll never forget the moment shortly after school started when she realized that I was a little too loud, a little too wild, and a little too different for the comfort level of the other kids and even our teacher. She stopped talking to me, but that didn't hurt as much as when she came over to my desk with her new crew of friends to make fun of the way I was coloring in a picture. "Look, y'all, she can't even stay in the lines. What a baby," she'd said. The eruption of laughter permeated the classroom as I sunk further and further into myself, building walls, and willing my ears to tune out the cruel heckling surrounding me. At six years old, my heart broke for the first time. Virginia continued to punish me for years after that, and I often longed for a way to make her stop.

When I was thirteen, I became obsessed with all the movies and TV shows about teenage witches. I loved the stories of friends getting together, practicing magic, and calling upon Mother Earth to help them kick ass. I was like, "Yep, that's for me." I secretly set up an altar in my bedroom with the stump of a candle, some pretty rocks, a tiny bird skull I found in the woods behind our house, and herbs from the neighbor lady's garden. I tried to emulate the witchy wardrobe and woman-of-mystery vibe I saw in the movies. I was always a fake-it-till-you-make-it kid. Like if I walked, talked, and appeared a certain way, I'd eventually end up being the thing I wanted to be: someone who was strong.

I convinced a group of girls at school to get into the whole witchy vibe with me. We all ate lunch together at the affectionately titled "outcast table," a group of kids that didn't have any friends to sit with at their designated lunch time. I think some sort of Moon, Earth, or energy day was happening, and I told everyone to dress in all black and meet me before school to do a ritual that coincided with the day. It was supposed to be a day to set your intention and draw power from the Earth. It was supposed to be fun, harmless.

When we all got to school, we sat in a circle outside and repeated a chant together. The surrounding leaves started swirling and then went toward a crowd of students—one of which was Virginia Freakin' Lovern, the queen of the bullies—and freaked them out. I felt a little rush of pleasure from that.

We went through our day much like every other day, but then at PE, things changed. When we walked into class, a small crowd of primarily popular kids was waiting for us. At first, I loved it. People were finally noticing me. The most popular girl in school and the bane of my existence, Virginia, walked right up to us, but instead of a warm greeting—and honestly, I don't know what I was expecting—she started calling us witches and some choice derogatory words. I stood my ground though. I didn't cower. I looked straight into her eyes; I saw fear there, and I liked it. I had found a way to have power over a bully. I felt strong and just a little wicked.

When things started to escalate, however, I did start to panic. The crowd of hecklers grew, and I began to wish that everyone would just leave me alone, leave us alone. They surrounded us. I could tell that the other girls were feeling scared. The crowd began pushing and shoving us, and Virginia got up in my face again. I kept repeating in my head over and over, "Just go away. Something make this stop, please."

Suddenly, bees started swarming around Virginia and her friends. I was relieved. I'd asked for help, and something had answered my plea. As Virginia began backing up, her eyes locked with mine. Terror and accusation stared back at me. As the bees circled closer to her, she started screaming and running away. Everyone, including my friends, looked at me with eyes wide as saucers. They thought I'd somehow caused the bee attack.

I honestly didn't know that I didn't. I mean, I was very into the idea of having some secret magic power inside me. But I didn't really believe in that possibility until that moment. It scared me. I was only thirteen, sheltered and small, and the first time I'd ever tried to remove the shackles of who I was and become who I wanted to be, something terrible happened. It didn't make everything better. It made everything worse.

I didn't really want to hurt Virginia. I'd initially just wanted her to know that I wasn't someone to be messed with. I wanted to be someone who wasn't ignored. Well, I got her attention, all right. All I wanted now was to go back to being a ghost, back to no one even knowing my name. Now, after everything spiraled out of control, all I wanted was for her to leave me alone.

The PE teacher blew her whistle and yelled to my three friends and me to follow her. Virginia had run to her crying; she'd been stung a couple of times. Big crocodile tears were dripping down her face. She said I'd made the bees sting her, that I was a witch, and that I was evil. Instead of the teacher looking at her like she was nuts, she looked at me with fear and apprehension. We were promptly sent to the principal's office.

My dad grew up in the same small town where we lived; even if no one really knew me, unfortunately, they did know him and his mood swings. My principal had been my dad's basketball coach back in the day at this very same school. The principal was very disappointed in me. He said

I should be thankful Virginia wasn't allergic to bees because she could've died. A touch dramatic, right? He was trying to justify my punishment. I don't think he *really* thought I'd sent the bees at Virginia, but he didn't like how we were all dressed in black and had caused mass hysteria after everyone had heard what I did in PE. He eyed me like I was a snake coiled in his path. We were in the Bible Belt, and everyone was slightly superstitious with a healthy fear of the unknown. He suspended me and told me I needed to go home and take the week to rethink my life and my friends and shape up or ship out. He said this would be my first and only strike and that the next time I landed in his office, he would expel me.

When my mom came to pick me up, I convinced her that everyone had just made a big deal out of nothing, and I think she believed me. She said she wasn't going to tell my dad, and she'd just make him think I was sick for the rest of the week. He worked the second shift, so it'd be easy for him not to know the difference. I could tell I'd disappointed her though, and I hated that. She made me throw away the little altar in my room. She'd noticed my witchy obsession, and I was pretty embarrassed.

Halfway through my suspension, I started having major anxiety about returning to school. There was no way I could face those kids again. They'd never let me live it down. I went to my mom, hysterically crying about it. I begged her not to make me go back. Coincidentally, a small private school had opened near our house, and I was enrolled by the end of the week. I don't even know how she convinced my dad; we were not a wealthy family. They made it work somehow. I knew then and there that no matter what, she always had my back, even when I was wrong.

I told no one why I'd left my old school. I tried not to think about the ability I may or may not have shown; I shut that down completely. I reinvented myself and started playing sports. The school was too small to have real cliques. There were only so many of us in each class, so you kind of had to be friendly to everyone. I was still a bit of a loner there, kept to myself, and flew under the radar. I locked away the part of myself that was curious about magic, mysteries, and the unknown. I sealed her away and tried to become someone else, someone normal.

It worked until it didn't. Things kind of fell apart for me after my mom passed away. She was my person, my rock, and I was adrift for a while. As I approached my late twenties, something stirred in me. It craved more than the endless loop I was riding: work, pay bills, eat, sleep, repeat. I moved away from our small town to the city and left my facade behind. I wanted to be me, whoever that was and whatever she looked like. I wanted to live in the light and be proud of who I was, weirdo or not. My mom would've wanted me to live like that. I wanted me to live like that. I didn't want to keep living my life in a quiet loop.

When I moved, I slowly started making friends. People liked me, loved me even. I got attention from girls and guys alike. It never ceased to shock me, especially the attention from the guys. I wasn't ugly; I never thought I was. It's just that I'd only ever really had one boyfriend. It ended badly, thwarting my desire to enter into another relationship.

Maybe it was the city, or maybe it was me being myself, weirdness and all, and people liked it. I felt a sense of capability that I'd never felt before.

And when I turned thirty, I just knew intensely that something inside of me was different. The locked-up thirteen-year-old girl who wanted to play with magic woke up. I cannot describe how I knew. It was just a feeling and a voice inside my head that told me to trust it. I was going to do great things. I was going to do something that scared me. I was going to create and be unstoppable. I really believed it too—until Heather was murdered, and I was arrested. My heart broken anew, like the old cracks I'd mended after my mother's death opened back up. And now once again, I felt adrift. I was an unmoored ship, floating off into the murky unknown.

I was in reality, however, sitting on Alison's couch, becoming one with the fabric, feeling all kinds of sorry for myself. I itched the skin around my ankle monitor. At that moment, I really couldn't fathom how my life could get any worse. The happy little life I'd been building in the city was shattered, and I didn't know how I was going to turn this around. I had to prove my innocence. The cops thought I was guilty, and it didn't seem like they were trying to find another suspect. It was up to me, but I was stuck under house arrest. I needed help.

CHAPTER 8

"Honey, I'm home," Alison's singsong voice called from the doorway.

I smiled at her flourishing entrance. "Hey, honey, what's for dinner?"

"I feel like I should ask you that. I'm the one working and bringing home that bacon. In your case, I guess it'd be like some soy-based fake bacon, right?" She teased me.

"Har-har, smart ass," I laughed.

"So, girl"—her gum smacking as she talked—"got some bad news," she said as she came to rest on the arm of the couch where I was sitting. I touched my chest where my mother's necklace normally lay. Alison noticed and paused, looking at me contemplatively.

"You know, Clarke, I still have the key to your place. I can sneak in and grab you some shit. I can be in and out so fast no would ever know." She smiled conspiratorially.

"Alison, I'll be back there in a few days." I was always thankful for Alison's inclination to lighten any potentially problematic situation. I could never stay down for long around her; she had a way of making me laugh through even the worst times.

"Well, babe, that's part of the bad news," she continued.

"I literally do not want any more bad news, Alison," I whined.

"Well, it's not that kind of bad news, girl. No one's dead."

I looked at her pointedly.

"No one else! Gosh, girl. Anyway," she rolled her eyes, "I just have to go out of town tomorrow. It's a last-minute hair show in New York, and the salon is requiring all of us to go, and I'm really excited because one of those weird phenomenons the news has been talking about just popped up there. The Hudson has a weird castle-looking thing sticking out of it near the Statue of Liberty."

"Okaaaay," I drawled. "That does sound pretty interesting. Well, I don't understand; that's good news, right? You'll have fun up there, and I can chill here by myself."

"Not the bad news, babe. Daddy says that your apartment is still an active crime scene—something about the missing murder weapon—anyway, he said they don't know when your place will be ready, so the cops want ya in temporary housing. I guess our roomie time has come to an end. After I talked to Daddy, I got a call from that sweet Officer Cain letting me know that someone will be by here to pick you up in the next few days."

"Ugh, I have to stay with some stranger from the police department?"

"Yeah, but it's just until your apartment is ready. I think. Or that's what Officer Cain said. She seemed to think your place would be ready soon. Either that, or she was just being nice." She shrugged.

"Well, I guess that's not too bad." I sighed, feeling super bummed. My shoulders slumped, and my face fell. I'd been wanting a little freedom, but not this. I'd taken my safe haven with Alison for granted.

"I know that face, girl. Ugh, I'm going to miss you too," she said as she pulled me in for a tight hug. "But if

Daddy's right, this whole thing should blow over soon, and everything will go back to normal."

"He's that hopeful about my case? Seriously?"

"Yeah, girl, seriously. You didn't do anything, duh, and he's like super great at his job, so ...," she said as she inspected a chip in her nail.

Buzz ... buzz. Alison's phone vibrated in her hand.

"Hey," she answered.

I listened to one side of the conversation.

"Yeah, she's still here. … Stop being such a dick. … She's leaving in like two days. … Ugh, fine, yeah, see you later."

"Um, was that Cody?" I asked worriedly.

"Yes, it was his assholeness." She rolled her eyes.

Cody was her boyfriend. I'd met him and the rest of their crew the same night I'd met Alison, but we didn't really get to know each other until a few weeks later when I'd finally given in to Alison's entreaties to hang out with her and her friends. I'd worn the cutest outfit I owned, really wanting them to like me. Alison had seemed so cool, and I wanted to impress her friends and feel like I fit in.

We'd met up at Cody's house, which smelled stale, like spilled alcohol and cigarettes. Everyone else had already gathered in the living room on various hodge-podge couches, watching some TV show.

"Clarke, this is the crew. Crew, Clarke."

"Hey, Clarke," Cody said as he rose from one couch and extended a hand. With his rugged, disheveled appearance, blue eyes, and dark-blonde hair, he reminded me of the guy everyone had a crush on in high school.

I reached out to shake his hand. He grasped my hand in his two clammy hands, holding me there. Was that … friendly? I pulled my hand back, took an empty seat on the edge of the couch, and inconspicuously wiped my hand off on my pants leg. Gross.

"Here, babe," Alison said as she brought in a glass of wine from the kitchen.

"Thank you," I replied as I grabbed the glass from her, and she took a seat next to me between me and her boyfriend.

Cody dropped an arm around her and smirked at me. "So, Clarke, Alison tells us you just moved here."

"Yeah, about six months now."

"Do you have a boyfriend?"

"Why would you ask her that?" Alison chided.

"Just curious, baby," he replied charmingly.

"No, I don't. I don't have a boyfriend, I mean."

"Surprising."

"Why is that surprising?" I asked and then finished my glass of wine. My nerves were already frayed by hanging out with new people, and his attention made it worse. I wondered if he was just like this or if I was reading too much into it. Alison didn't seem too annoyed or alarmed by his attention toward me, so I assumed it was normal.

"You want some more, girl?" she said when she noticed my empty glass.

"Sure, thank you."

When she got up to collect my glass and take it into the kitchen to refill it, Cody had smacked her ass. She turned to chastise him, but he smiled at her suggestively, and she just smiled back.

"It's surprising because you're fucking hot," Cody said when Alison left the room.

"Huh, oh, um, thank you," I said, stumbling over my words. I knew I was pretty but often felt uncomfortable being complimented. I'd lost a few friends over the years when their crush in school would like me and not them. I'd come home crying over another lost friend and my mom would pull me into her lap and stroke my hair and assure me that they were only jealous of me. I'd always hated that explanation and would try to stifle my features so that I wouldn't be noticed as much. I wore baggy clothes or sometimes two sports bras to hide my ample curves that arrived before the other girls my age. I didn't want them to be jealous. I wanted their friendship. So I thought if I could do something to make the boys stop noticing me, then it wouldn't be an issue anymore. I especially felt uncomfortable when my new best friend's boyfriend complimented me. I could envision the animosity building all over again with Alison resenting me and eventually abandoning me like all the rest. I shifted nervously on the couch, willing Alison to come back and hoping no one else in the room noticed his compliment.

"You should hang out with us more often," he continued. "Wouldn't mind seeing you again."

"Umm …"

Alison interrupted my reply, returning with my full wine glass.

"Thank you," I said, taking the glass from her.

"Sure, girl," she replied, cozying up to Cody.

My anxiety hitched, and my inner monologue went into overdrive: Did she say that with a bit of ice in her tone, or did I imagine it? Had she heard him? Fuck. Calm down, Clarke. You're obviously reading too much into everything because you're nervous. Alison isn't mad at you. Cody was just being nice. From the outside it had probably looked like I'd just taken a deep breath and sipped my wine while getting caught up in the characters and drama on TV instead of overanalyzing the exchange.

I shook myself out of my Cody-induced reverie. "His assholeness? Did you guys have a fight? Is he not okay that I'm here? I thought you said the crew pooled their money to help bail me out. Why would he be upset that I'm here?"

"Ugh, girl, okay. Well, the crew didn't exactly pull their money together. I stretched the truth so you wouldn't feel bad."

"How stretched, Alison?" I asked warily.

"Like, fine, so I begged Daddy to loan you—I mean me—the money to bail you out." When I continued to stare shockingly at her, she continued. "Girl, I'm sorry. No one wanted me to let you stay here. Like Cody was hella pissed about it. My dad took some extra buttering up for it, but he caved in the end like he always does," she said as she inspected her chipped nail again.

"Why did you lie to me?" I really didn't like being lied to. Alison was always so blunt and honest. It was the thing I loved most about her. You knew where you stood with her—no surprises.

"That," she said as she pointed her finger at me, "that freaking look on your face is why. I didn't want you to know."

"Why didn't they want me here?" I asked, feeling small and self-conscious.

"Well, duh, Clarke, they were just concerned that I had someone living with me who is accused of *murrr-derrr*," she said as she rolled her eyes again. She'd drawn out the word "murder" into two long syllables like you would when teaching a child how to say it for the first time.

I was getting pissed. Defensive. These people were supposed to be my closest friends. I felt sick. They didn't think I killed Heather, right? Fuck, this is why I didn't let people in. They lied, manipulated, hid things, and I really hated that.

"Look," Alison said, "I'm sorry I didn't tell you. I was just trying to protect you. You've been through enough. They'll come around. They love you. Cody loves you too. Everyone loves you, girl, duh. It's kind of annoying," an unreadable expression lit her face before she flashed one of her thousand-watt smiles. "I know you didn't kill anyone. So do they. They just freaked out, okay, and my dad doesn't count. He doesn't know you, and he's just being overprotective. Fuck 'em, okay? Don't get all worked up. Do one of those breathing exercises or something."

"Okay, fine, I understand why you kept it from me. Please never do it again. You know me and my trust issues. Dishonesty is a big trigger for me."

"Honest Abe here from now on, girl. Promise," she said as she saluted me.

I grinned at that.

"Now, let's get drunk off cheap wine and watch something sappy!"

How could I say no to that?

"Sounds good to me. One condition though."

"Sure, babe, anything."

"You've got to promise to get a picture of this castle thing for me when you go to New York."

"I think I can manage that," she said with a wink.

***

"Ugh … my head." I woke up to a splitting headache from all the cheap red wine Alison and I had consumed last night. I felt a body stir next to me.

"Clarke, seriously, girl, why are you being so loud right now?" Alison grumbled.

I opened my eyes to see we had passed out on the couch together, our bodies and legs intertwined. We were still fully clothed in our jeans and everything. No wonder I felt so confined and stiff when I woke up.

"Alison," I said as I nudged her, "go get us some water and headache medicine."

"Girl, whisper voice, puh-lease. And, no, you go get it. Why is it so damn bright in here anyway? Go turn off the lights."

"You left the curtains open. And it's bright because it's morning."

"Fuck, I've got to get ready to leave for New York. What time is it? Do you think I missed my flight?"

My head throbbed as I heard a loud thump. Alison had tumbled to the floor in a heap.

"Shit, oh, too fast, too fast, the spins, oh, girl, I'm gonna …," Alison trailed off as she covered her mouth and ran to her bathroom.

"Yep, she's going to vomit," I said. "Shit, Clarke, stop thinking about vomiting." I retched. Cupping my mouth, I ran to the kitchen sink since Alison was occupying the only bathroom. I had no choice but to upchuck into the sink.

Unfortunately, our drunk asses had left our red wine-stained glasses in the sink along with a cutting board full of remnants from the copious amounts of cheese we'd consumed.

I washed my face and busied myself with washing the dishes free of wine and cheese residue and puke.

As I pulled a clean glass from the cabinet and proceeded to fill it with water so I could get some headache medicine in my body, I could hear the tornado of Alison's hurried packing. She was chaos on a typical day, but late Alison was a wonder to behold.

She fled from her bedroom with a giant pink suitcase almost as big as her, a sizeable floral-printed carry-on duffel, and a smaller designer crossbody bag that was peppered with logos.

"Damn, girl, aren't you only going to be gone for like two days?"

"Yeah, girl, but you know me. I always need all the things."

I chuckled. She did always overpack, but this seemed extreme, even for her. "Okay, don't forget to call me when you get there to tell me you're safe."

"Yes, Mom," Alison said as she rolled her eyes.

"Har-har, but I mean it."

"I said I would! Chill, girl."

She came over to hug me goodbye and squeezed me hard.

"Alison, I can't breathe."

"Sorry, girl, just, um, I'm going to miss you."

"I'll miss you too, but I'll see you soon, okay?"

"Yeah, okay ... bye, Clarke," she said with a note of sadness in her voice. I guess we had been having fun playing roomies the couple of days that I'd been here, but I didn't realize she would be this sad to leave me.

"Bye! Have fun!" I called as she wheeled her luggage outside to wait for her car service to the airport.

I grabbed my water, brought it back to the couch, and curled up in the blankets, planning on staying there all day to nurse my epic hangover. I switched the TV on and turned to the news channel.

"A giant skeleton of what appears to be a serpent-like creature has washed up on the shore of Wrightsville Beach," said the reporter. "Marine biologists and archeology teams are on the scene conducting tests to determine the creature's origin. Authorities are skeptical and think it could be a large art sculpture, much like the other phenomena that have popped up seemingly out of nowhere."

The image on TV was amazing. It really looked like the ancient skeleton of an enormous sea monster. Wrightsville Beach was so close. I so wished I wasn't in this situation; I would have loved to drive and see it.

A wave of melancholy hit me as I changed the channel and sank deeper into the blankets.

CHAPTER 9

You know when you have a feeling that something terrible is about to happen? Like you're waiting all week for a piano to drop out of someone's apartment building on your head, or you feel like you forgot to turn off your straightener or to blow out a candle at home, and you just know your whole house has likely burned to ashes? I'd felt like that for the few days I'd been at Alison's—full of buzzing anxiety. She had doted on me when she wasn't working, practically hand feeding me all my favorite vegan snacks. She'd stocked up on all my favorite foods, bought me some new books, and done everything she could to keep me as happy as possible. Even after finding Heather dead, being charged with her murder, and spending a few days in jail, the time I spent under house arrest with Alison had been surprisingly normal.

I'd learned I no longer had a job—no tremendous surprise there. Even if the family I'd worked for thought I was innocent, I was under house arrest for however long, so they couldn't hold my job for me. They also couldn't keep me on after I was charged because of the sheer optics of it. Of course, I understood; I would've fired me too. I wasn't even upset with them. So why did I feel doom looming over my head?

The day after Alison left, around lunchtime, I heard someone knock on the door. I got up from my couch nest and walked over to the front door. I looked through the peephole and gasped. A man dressed in all black—suit, shirt, tie, and aviator sunglasses was staring straight back at me through the fisheye lens. How creepy! I knew he couldn't see me, but it was unnerving, especially with how the lens warped the image.

I figured it had to be the officer who was supposed to come and collect me. "Shit," I mumbled as I snuck another peep, "why didn't they call me? I haven't packed any of my stuff."

I swung the door open.

"Hi, ma'am, I'm …"

I didn't quite catch the rest of his introduction because, holy fuck, this guy was hot. He was tall, slim, and fit. His hair was longish, about shoulder length, and was pulled back neatly at the nape of his neck. Yummy, I thought—and then, shit, shit, I wasn't expecting *him*. I'd pictured someone like the gross old man I'd met when I'd first gotten to the prison or a female like Officer Cain or Officer Luck. When had I last showered? Friday? Was I even wearing deodorant? Fuck. He was standing in front of me staring, so there was no way to do the quick underarm smell test. Shit, how long have we been standing here like this, I thought, staring and not talking? Well, he'd at least introduced himself … I think … shit. I'd been too tongue-tied to respond or even notice.

The stranger smirked, "Miss Carpenter?"

He reached into his pocket, retrieved a business card, and handed it to me.

"Yeah, yes, that's me," I replied and extended my hand to take the business card from him. Our fingers brushed, and a slight tremor went through my arm.

"Like I was saying, I'm Detective Taylor. I believe the department informed you that someone would be by to transport you to temporary housing while your condo is still unavailable."

"Oh, yes, they did. I'm so sorry. Yes, would you like to come in?"

"Yes, but we need to be on our way."

"Oh, sure. I have to pack and would love to shower quickly if I can. I didn't realize what day it was and wasn't sure when they would be sending someone."

He seemed to survey my appearance then. His gaze traveled all the way from my greasy hair to my bare feet. Shit, I thought, I must look like three pegs past a hot mess. I'd thought I'd get some warning before being carted off, but I guess they couldn't call me if I didn't have a phone that worked.

"Hmm … yes, I see." He seemed to consider my dilemma while his gaze raked up and down my body once more. Something about this guy made me feel exposed, like he could see straight through to my soul with those aviator glasses. "You seem to have a weird stench coming from you. Maybe it's all the crumbs on your wrinkled shirt? I'm hoping that isn't just how you smell." He smirked with that shit-eating grin. He was joking, right? "I'm joking, Miss Carpenter. Quickly then. Shower and pack. We leave in twenty minutes," he said, looking at this watch.

My cheeks flamed red, and I rushed toward the bathroom. As I took in my appearance in the mirror, I felt the weirdest feeling of familiarity, like I'd met Detective Taylor before. Maybe I'd seen him in passing in the police department. Much to my chagrin, even if he was kidding about the stench, he was probably right. I looked terrible. What the hell was I wearing? A huge, oversized T-shirt that went to my knees, likely one that Cody had left here, and no pants. I was so embarrassed that my cheeks went from red to purple, and I could feel my chest heating as it started to form red splotches. Why did he have to be so hot? I hadn't bothered changing my clothes or showering in days. A quick armpit inspection confirmed that I did, in fact, smell. Fucking embarrassing. I sure knew how to make an impression.

I untangled my hair from its perch on top of my head, peeled off my crusty shirt, and got undressed. Twenty minutes later, I was clean, dressed, and had halfway dried my wavy hair. Not wanting to don another one of Cody's shirts that Alison had confiscated, I was left with only one option: one of her too-tight and risqué ones. Fabulous.

"Finally, you are ... presentable," he stumbled over his words as his eyes landed on my cleavage, which was spilling out of Alison's low-cut T-shirt. He cleared his throat and raised his eyes. I could have sworn a tinge of pink dusted his cheeks. "I was afraid the dirt was permanently stuck to you, but voilà, you can be rendered clean," he joked, trying to cover up the fact that he had definitely checked me out.

"Seriously?"

He sighed, "Apologies, another joke. I'm afraid I'm not very funny."

"Uh, yeah, no worries, dude—sir! Um, Detective Taylor, sorry." Why was I so nervous? This was getting ridiculous. Maybe it was because he'd taken off his sunglasses, and his dark-brown eyes were so sexy that I swore the temperature in the room had increased.

"You may address me as Detective Taylor, detective, or Haywood."

"Okay, Detective Taylor." I stuck my hand out. "Clarke. Nice to meet you."

He eyed my hand like he didn't know what a handshake was. I grasped his hand in mine to shake it and felt an electric shock that started from our clasped hands all the way through my body. Haywood looked at me with surprise, and something else flickered in his gaze before he quickly schooled his features into an indifferent mask.

"What the fuck was that?!" I yelled, jerking my hand out of his.

"I don't know what you mean, Miss Carpenter. Have you never felt static shock before?"

"Yes, of course, I've felt a static shock before. That was different. That was—what was that?"

"Again, I'm not sure what you are asking me," he deadpanned.

"You know what? Never mind. Maybe I'm going insane. Maybe I didn't just feel like I was electrocuted. Whatever. I'm going to go pack a few things, and then we can get on with this charade." I stormed off in the direction of Alison's room to borrow a bag, so I could pack. She wouldn't mind if I borrowed a few of her clothes to get me by. I opened drawer after drawer, finding almost all of them empty. Damn, she wasn't kidding about needing all the things, but luckily, she'd left a couple essentials behind that would work for me.

When I emerged from the bedroom, the detective was sitting at Alison's kitchen table. He stood up, pulled out one of the chairs, and indicated that he wanted me to sit down.

"I thought we were leaving," I questioned.

"Come sit, please."

I walked over and plopped down. Officer Taylor bent down and took my foot into his lap. Goosebumps traveled up my body as his hands grazed my sock-covered foot.

"Um, what are you doing?" I questioned with alarm while trying to hide the shiver of excitement at his contact.

"I will be removing your ankle monitor since I've convinced the authorities that while you're in my care, you will not run off and get into more mischief." He leaned into my personal space. "I can count on you to not run off, can't I, Miss Carpenter?"

My breath caught at his proximity. He was handsome and exotic in that way that you knew he wasn't from around here. He did have a slight accent, but I couldn't place it. He smelled like spring dew, fresh flowers, and something wholly masculine.

Oh my god, I thought, why am I smelling him like a fucking creeper? Get yourself together, Clarke. I sat back in the chair, feeling crowded and flushed.

"It's Clarke," I said.

"Pardon?"

"Please call me Clarke."

He nodded in response.

"Okay, Clarke." Oh shit, I liked how he said my name. A tingling feeling ran all the way up my spine.

He lifted his full dark lashes up as his gaze met mine. "I can trust you not to run away if I take this off, correct?"

"Of course, Detective Taylor," I said in an embarrassingly breathy tone. Whew, my mind raced through images of him taking other things off. Shit, stop it. Luckily, he seemed to not notice how flustered I was.

"Haywood," he said.

"Huh?"

"You may call me Haywood if you wish."

"Oh, okay, Haywood." Gosh, why did this guy make me so nervous, and what kind of name was Haywood Taylor? It sounded like some Southern daytime drama actor's name.

A companionable silence passed between us as he worked on removing my ankle monitor.

"I do not think you killed Heather Dunn," he said.

"Huh? Really?" I hadn't been expecting that statement at all.

"I've been going over this case, and I've investigated you as well. My gut tells me you're not a killer. I'd like to help you clear your name and find out who is really at fault."

"You're serious? Why would you want to help me?"

"Other than it is my duty to bring the guilty party to justice as I am investigating this murder?" He eyed me incredulously while creasing a brow.

"Oh, yeah, right? That makes sense." Duh, he was a detective. Of course, he wanted to find the actual killer if it wasn't me. That was his job.

"When we get you settled, we can go over the case files, and maybe you can see something we missed. You knew her, after all, you might see something out of place."

"Oh, sure, yes, I'd like that." This was an interesting turn of events. I certainly wanted the chance to clear my name and needed the help. Haywood was turning out to be most unexpected in more ways than one.

After removing my ankle monitor, he sat my foot back down and got up from the table.

"We really must be going," he said as he grabbed my bag, glanced again at his watch, and eyed the room nervously.

"I'm ready when you are."

Without a word, he headed to the door. I followed quickly.

He approached a black car and opened the passenger side door.

"After you," he said, holding the door open for me. What a gentleman. With manners and looks, I was a goner.

"Thank you," I replied as I slid into the front seat and clipped the seat belt closed.

Haywood walked around to the back, opened the trunk, and placed my bag inside before sliding into the driver's seat and starting the car.

As we headed out of the city, I relaxed a bit and leaned my head against the headrest.

CHAPTER 10

Strong, callused hands gripped the sides of my face as jewel green eyes bored into mine. Soft, full lips drew me in. I lifted my hands and grasped fists full of hair, drawing our heads closer as our tongues began to dance. It still wasn't close enough. Warmth spread from my lips to every part of my body. I was on fire—body and soul. We became a pretzel of arms and legs as a frenzied need took over. When we broke apart, we turned our heads to face one another. I struggled to memorize the face that stared back at me ....

"Clarke?"

"Hmmm?" Someone was waking me up from a seriously sexy dream. Sea-green eyes haunted me as I peeled mine open. I'd seen those eyes before. Why couldn't I ever remember his face? Ugh, so frustrating. I turned and saw brown eyes sparkling back at me.

"What were you dreaming about, Clarke?" Haywood asked, his eyebrow lifting suggestively.

"Nothing!" I blushed. "None of your business! Sorry … I … I didn't mean to fall asleep. Are we there yet?" Haywood had been driving me to my temporary abode. I must have dozed off after we left Alison's.

"Yes, we are almost there. That, however, isn't the reason for waking you," he said, smiling coyly.

"Aaaand … are you going to tell me the reason?"

"I was only being courteous. You were making interesting sounds over there and speaking of unmentionable things. Inappropriate things," he expounded.

"I thought it might embarrass you to continue what I can only guess was a very intriguing dream." He looked at me pointedly.

Oh. My. God. I was so embarrassed. And Haywood was teasing me again.

"Um, yeah, sorry about that. I'm not a peaceful sleepier. I'm pretty vocal."

That earned me another pointed glance and an eyebrow raise.

"When I dream, vocal when I dream, I mean. I sometimes talk in my sleep. Is it hot in here? Can we turn on the AC?"

"Of course." He reached over to open the air vents on my side of the car, brushing my arm. Much to my embarrassment, chills broke out on my arm.

"Thank you."

"My pleasure."

Yeah, mine too, I thought. Fuck, why am I so affected by the proximity of this guy? He's a cop, well, detective. He is the definition of off-limits. Down, girl!

Haywood leaned in and tucked a hair behind my ear. I flinched back slightly. He eyed me a moment and then, "We are here Clarke," he whispered.

My eyes bugged out. "Huh?" I hadn't even noticed the car had come to a stop.

"I said we are here," he repeated and moved to exit the car. He tried to conceal the slight smile on his face but failed. Apparently, he was aware of his effect on me and was amused by it. How wonderful.

Even though I was embarrassed by my actions, my body still shuddered at that small amount of contact. I was

in trouble. It'd been a minute since the last time I'd had
sex. And I wasn't in a position to knock those cobwebs
off—with anyone let alone the detective on my case. I had
shit to do. My name to clear. My treacherous body needed
to chill the hell out. I blamed the sexy dream, not the long-
haired, sexy detective who was motioning for me to get out
of the car. Fuck, this was not going to work.

We walked up to a yellow, wood-sided house. It had a
wraparound porch littered with old rocking chairs.
Haywood unlocked the white front door and held it open
for me. It was a one-story house with an open-plan living
room and kitchen and several rooms off a lone hallway. It
was homey; it felt comfortable.

"Feel free to pick whatever bedroom you'd like. There
are two."

"Oh, yes, thank you. I'll go set my bag down in one of
them then."

"When you're ready, meet me in the kitchen, and we
can look over the case files together," He called as I walked
toward one of the bedrooms.

"Sounds great. I'll be right back." I answered.

I sat my things down on a bed with a floral-patterned
comforter. This place was way too lovely to be government
housing. I wondered if this could be Haywood's home. If it
was, did he live alone? I doubted very much that he had
picked out the décor. Everything had a feminine flair to it—
pastel colors, florals—and was neat as a pin. I supposed
Haywood could have those tastes as well. He just seemed
so masculine and rugged. The environment in this house
was light and airy, with a touch of whimsy. The style of his
head-to-toe black outfit was such a contrast to the bright,

relaxed state of the home. No, I decided, probably just a prettily decorated rental house. I'd imagined we were headed to one of those cold and bleak safe houses you always saw in crime shows. I guess they were just fiction; they probably all looked normal like this one. I sighed and checked my appearance in the mirror above the dresser next to the bed, patted down the frizz of my hair, wiped away a few mascara smears courtesy of my nap in the car, and left the room to join Haywood.

***

Almost two days went by, and my worry grew. Heather's murderer was still out there, and even with Haywood's help, we hadn't made a ton of progress.

I kept my distance from Haywood as much as possible except for when we were looking over the case files. I didn't trust my libido around him, not that he would entertain any of my advances. He was professional; I was just work for him.

Besides, sex was the last thing on my mind while poring over gruesome photos of the crime scene. It was the first time I'd seen Heather's dead body in the light. The killer had stabbed her only once and straight through her heart. Haywood said whoever had killed her had been strong. To get to the heart from that angle, you had to crack all the bones surrounding it, protecting it. I'd never known or had a reason to think about it until now. With this knowledge, I felt a little more secure about proving my innocence. I was strong, but not that strong. He also said that this method most likely meant that it was a crime of passion, that someone must have been fueled by anger to kill her like that, and that she probably knew her killer. That was a little disheartening since it seemed to me that I was the only person in Heather's life.

The next day, he informed me he was going to go take another look at the crime scene. I wasn't invited. I was stuck alone again in a random house in the middle of nowhere. My only comfort was the very soft and comfortable couch. I think I pictured this whole crime sleuthing differently. I thought it'd be a bit more active.

I guess Haywood wouldn't be fulfilling any of my buddy cop fantasies anytime soon. My stomach rumbled, alerting me that it was lunchtime. As I perused the kitchen, I found that it was stocked with lots of my favorite foods. Either Haywood and I had the exact same taste in food and the same food allergies, or he'd somehow known what I would like. I was too hungry to contemplate the weirdness of that. Instead, I grabbed as many treats as I could carry and shuffled back to the couch in the living room.

I was in the middle of snack heaven when Haywood came barreling in through the front door.

"Get packed; we're leaving!" he exclaimed, looking frantic and ruffled.

"What's going on? Did you find something?"

"Yes! No! I don't know. We must move to another house. You must get up. We have to leave now. No time to explain," he said breathlessly.

I rushed around collecting my things and all the snacks Haywood had bought me. Luckily, I'd showered and dressed earlier, so I didn't have to waste any time. I hadn't seen Haywood so disheveled, and his urgency made me not question him until we were in the car and well on our way.

He looked like he'd just seen a ghost.

"Haywood," I probed. "Can you tell me what happened? Why did we have to leave? Are we not safe? What did you find?"

Taking a deep breath, he turned to face me and then turned back to the road. He took another deep breath.

"I do not know how to tell you this, Clarke. You will find out either way, but …"

"Oh, my fuck, Haywood, I'm freaking out now. Please, just tell me before I lose it."

He took a third deep breath. "Alison is missing …." He paused. "Clarke, I am so sorry. They are saying you are somehow involved."

"What? Wait, what do you mean Alison is missing? You're wrong, Haywood. She is out of town on a work trip in New York. This can't be right."

"They are saying she never made it to New York. Her father reported her missing this morning. No one has seen her since she left you at her apartment."

My stomach hollowed out, and I sank deeper into the seat of the car.

That was almost three days ago. I didn't know what to think. Alison couldn't be missing. There had to be a logical explanation here. This could not be happening.

"Wait, why are we leaving? Shouldn't you be taking me back to prison? Leaving makes me look guilty! This makes no sense, Haywood. We have to go back."

"Yes, if we would have stayed, I'm sure they would have brought you in for more questioning and kept you there. There would be no chance of bail this time, Clarke."

"So … you are helping me?"

"Yes, I am helping you."

"Why? Why would you do that? I don't understand. You barely know me."

"I cannot explain. What I can say is that I don't think you killed Heather, and since you've been with me for most of the time Alison's been missing, I do not think you are involved with her disappearance either."

That seemed logical, but I still didn't understand why he was helping me. Who was I to him? He would get in trouble, right? My mind was spinning.

"I don't know what to say to that. Where are we going?"

"You'll see." He paused. "Somewhere safe."

He seemed to be done talking, and I needed a minute to collect my thoughts. My temples ached, and I sighed. This was not good. Alison could not be missing. There had to be another explanation. "Maybe she ran off with Cody to Vegas and got married?" I mused. "She's impulsive like that. Yes, that's it. She's off somewhere on some hair-brained adventure and didn't tell anyone." I refused to accept that something nefarious had happened to her.

"Okay, well, it's too damn quiet in this car, and I need a distraction." I reached for the radio and turned it on.

"Clarke, wait!" he said, trying to get me not to turn on the radio.

"Another phenomenon has been spotted. This time a giant castle has popped up in the middle of the Indian

Ocean," said the radio news reporter. "And now breaking news: authorities say they have found Alison Villareal's body behind the Uptown salon where she worked. Villareal was reported missing just this morning. No details were released on the cause of death. An APB has been issued for the primary suspect, Clarke Carpenter. Last week, Carpenter was accused of murdering her roommate, Heather Dunn. She was released on bail and was under house arrest in Alison Villareal's home before both women went missing. Authorities have refused to speculate whether we might be dealing with a serial killer like the Taco Bell Strangler, who murdered eleven women in our area in the 1990s. Others are calling the deaths of Heather Dunn and Alison Villareal the Roommate Murders. Hopefully, the murderer will be caught soon and brought to justice. Please call the Crime Stoppers tip line if you have any information pertaining to the crime or Clarke Carpenter's whereabouts."

"Haywood …," I croaked. "What the hell? You said she was missing. What is this? What is happening?" I sobbed as a tear escaped my eye. I rarely cried. I hadn't even cried when Heather was found dead, not even when I was losing my mind in prison. I hadn't really cried since … since Mom.

"Clarke, I'm so sorry. I didn't know. I swear. Her father reported her missing early this morning. They must have looked for her right away. I promise I did not know," he said as he covered my hand with his.

I moved out of his grasp. Alison? Dead? No, not Alison. Please no.

Alison was … dead?

A voice in my head was screaming. My breath halted. Someone had filled my ears with cotton, and beads of sweat built on my temples and hairline. My mouth went dry as my heart froze. Time stopped. Everything stopped.

CHAPTER 11

Haywood

The car stopped as if I'd slammed on brakes. Clarke and I were thrown forward. I braced against the steering wheel, my head secure against the headrest. Clarke had not been so lucky. Leaning back in her seat, she clasped her forehead with her hands. She must have hit her head.

I looked around us. We were on a rural road, and I was thankful that no one was around or behind us. A collision would have complicated things further.

As I looked around, I blinked once, then twice, not believing what I was seeing. Ice had formed on the car windows like morning frost. I looked to my left and saw a bee frozen in mid-flight right outside the window. Past the bee, a tree looked like it was leaning to the right. But no, I realized, the limbs were caught to one side as they had been blowing in the wind. There was no sound. Only stillness.

I looked to my right at Clarke. She had not removed her hands from her face and was rocking back and forth. Clarke's reaction to Alison's death had stopped time and everything around us. It was the only explanation.

I knew when I'd been tasked to watch over her that there was something more to my assignment. I was meant to observe her, keep her safe, and then more recently, I'd been asked to retrieve her. I'd been so captivated by the creature next to me I'd almost lost sight of my mission. I'd overseen her safety in this world since she was a child. It was an honor bestowed upon me by the highest ruler of my realm, my sovereign, Solana. Clarke had grown into such a breathtaking, vivacious woman. If you ignored her crass language and behavior, she was the most incredible creature I'd ever encountered. She wasn't aware of what she'd just done.

Until recently, she had never been able to see or hear me. Obviously, her powers were starting to awaken. I reached out to touch her shoulder. The irony that I could touch her now was not lost on me, nor had her small reactions to my touch gone unnoticed. Empathy was one of my gifts, and the rushes of Clarke's erotic feelings were driving me to distraction. It would have been wrong to act on any of my own impulses, especially since she thought I was oblivious to her feelings. I needed to push all of these thoughts out of my head and make sure she was okay.

"Clarke … Clarke, are you … are you okay?"

My voice seemed to break through to her. The car rumbled to life, and everything around us resumed its forward motion.

She dropped her hands from her face, looking disoriented. She was likely concussed. I reached out with my senses and felt … nothing. Hollowness. A void had opened inside her. It felt cold—cold and dark. She didn't respond further, so I resumed driving.

The news about Alison's death had extinguished a light in her. It filled me with a deep desire to do something, anything, to comfort her. But words stuck in my mouth, my tongue unable to form any sentiment. We rode in silence.

She continued to stare out the window, letting the world pass her by.

I remained grateful that she was unaware of what she'd just done. I wasn't ready to explain. Of course, I would when the time came. For now, however, allowing her to grieve the loss of her friend was the priority.

CHAPTER 12

Clarke

I felt nothing as we drove for what seemed like hours. I was numb. I was wrong when I thought I'd hit rock bottom while sitting in prison for Heather's murder. This. This was my undoing.

Alison, my best friend, my first real friend, changed my life in the best possible way when we met. She burst into my life and heart despite my protests and despite all the walls I'd built to keep people out. Her smile, her laugh, her energy, even her stupid gum made my whole life brighter. In her, I knew true companionship for the first time. I learned what love felt like outside the mother-child bond. She wasn't just my best friend; in a short six months, she'd become my family, the only family I had left, and now she was gone. I felt truly alone in this world.

I'd felt similar to this when my mom died. But for some reason, this was so much worse. After Mom died, I'd resigned myself to living a life without my person. She was my soulmate, a part of me, and I didn't feel whole without her. Then Alison came along and made me think that maybe we get more than one soulmate in this lifetime, more than one chance to feel whole. She made me feel like I didn't need or even want to be alone anymore. She saw me and loved me just as my mom had.

I couldn't move on from this. I was done. They might as well take me to jail and give me the death penalty. What was the point of fighting? What was the point of anything? It was like every time I found a small sliver of joy in this world, something took it from me. Everything had been ripped from me: my Mom, Heather, and now Alison. If I'd had the power to shut myself off and just cease to exist, I would have exercised it in that moment. I wanted to escape, not just the situation, but my own skin, my own mind, my existence.

I turned and looked at Haywood. Conflict whirled as his brows pinched. What was he thinking? Was he regretting helping me?

I heard the turn light clicking as the car pulled onto a gravel road. We eventually emerged from a canopy of leaf-bare trees surrounded by bigger evergreens into a clearing with a small log-timbered cabin in the center. I allowed Haywood to take my hand and lead me into the house. He deposited me at the small table in the kitchen, instructing me not to move while he grabbed our bags. Moving was the least of what I wanted to do. I sat there like a vacant doll until I felt hands on my face and a damp cloth on my forehead. I winced as pain shot through my skull. Apparently, I *could* feel something, even if it was pain.

Memories and words flashed slowly. *"Alison is dead. ... The primary suspect, Clarke Carpenter ... Roommate Murders."* Then a nothingness and a crash. Did we wreck? Was I not wearing my seat belt? I'd hit my head, and now I was bleeding.

Haywood had turned my chair away from the table and pulled a chair up to mine for better access to survey and clean my wound. He was gently dabbing it with a washcloth. My blurry eyes found his worried ones. I took in his handsome face and found kindness there. He was essentially a stranger to me, but I felt such a pull to him. I trusted him. Something about him was familiar, and it was comforting. I couldn't explain it. And I found I didn't want to.

I was so cold. The kind of cold that seeps into your bones and kills you. And he was so warm. I leaned into the heat pulsing from his hand as it grazed my forehead.

What had I just been wanting? An escape? Yes, that was it. All thoughts fled my head as I let instinct take over. I reached up and took his hand from my face. He looked startled by my touch.

His alarm quickly turned into something else. Desire. Electricity sang between us, and this time he didn't look away or try to explain away the sensation. I knew we both felt it when our eyes locked.

We reached for each other simultaneously, drawing our faces inches apart. Haywood hesitated slightly, giving me a moment to protest what was about to happen. "I want this. I need this," I assured him. He smiled softly and leaned in to capture my lips.

His kiss was so sweet, so soft and sensual, but not as refined and gentle as I'd imagined it would be. And even through all the chaos, I had definitely imagined it. Instead, it had a distinct edge to it, a sort of barely leashed desperation. This is exactly what I needed. To stop thinking and drowning in emotions. To sink into the sensations my body could produce with the right motivation. To lose myself in Haywood.

I kissed him back then, deepening the kiss with a nudge of my tongue. Haywood startled again, but only slightly as he returned my nudge with fervor. His hands went around my waist and slid down to where my ass met the wooden chair. He grasped me and stood, lifting me like I weighed nothing, and carried me toward what I assumed was a bedroom. I wrapped my legs around him, feeling the evidence that he was just as affected by me as I was by him. My body thawed with his proximity, if only temporarily. We never broke kissing and touching as Haywood deposited me on the bed and climbed on top of me. I loved the weight of him; I felt warmth return to my cold, hard heart. I knew this was only a temporary escape from reality, but I'd take what I could get. As our clothes disappeared around the room, we escaped together in a moment of pure, liberating release.

***

I woke up on a blanket under the most enormous tree I'd ever seen. It looked just like the Angel Tree I had visited once with my mom when we were on vacation at the coast. The air smelled like freshly baked pastries. It was crisp, and as I breathed it in, I felt renewed and energized.

I sat up and gasped. As far as I could see, everything was covered in snow except the small patch of earth under the tree where I was. A distinct circle surrounded me and the blanket I was sitting on. I blinked at the brightness of the sun reflecting off the beautiful white terrain. I loved snow. It rarely snowed in the South. But when it did, everything would shut down, the world became quiet, and for one glorious day, we are all children again. We would eat it, sled in it, throw it, and make sculptures with it.

I stood up and saw a small stone village sitting off in the distance. I felt a sense of homecoming. I knew I'd never been here before—I knew it—but something about that place was wholly familiar. Sleep overcame me, and I was again lying on the softest blanket I'd ever felt. I closed my eyes, feeling settled, content, and at peace ....

I was freezing. That's all I could think as I stirred awake. I felt unsettled, frazzled, knocked off my axis. As the grogginess started to ebb from my body, I opened my eyes and realized that I was sitting in a chair in the living room wrapped very tightly in a blanket and then became very aware that I was naked underneath. I had no idea how I'd gotten here; I'd fallen asleep in bed with Haywood. Haywood who was now crouched to my right staring at me, concern etched on his handsome face.

"What in the actual fuck is going on?" I murmured sleepily.

"I'm sorry, but a snowstorm came through last night. The temperature dropped, and the heater broke. You were freezing when I woke up, and you wouldn't rouse. I started the fire in the hearth, so the house is already warming up, but I was afraid to let you carry on in your state. Clarke, you were barely breathing, and you were like ice. Are you okay?" He asked as he reached for me.

"I think so. I'm freezing now and I can't move, where are my clothes?"

Haywood flushed. "I apologize for undressing you, but your clothes were damp, and I was afraid they were hindering your body from warming up."

"That's just … bizarre. I never even get cold. It's the South. I barely even wear a jacket here," I felt disoriented and dizzy, and I couldn't stop shaking.

"We are in the mountains now, Clarke. Temperatures dropped to single digits last night."

"That makes sense. Sorry, I didn't mean to scare you. It was just a bizarre way to wake up, ya know."

"Of course. No need to apologize. I'm just grateful you are okay."

I thought I was ok, but I felt so strange and was weirdly self-conscious of being naked. Which after last night didn't make sense. Somehow, in the light of day, I was feeling some regret for basically jumping a stranger. Well, not a stranger, but what did I even know about Haywood? I'd been so relieved to have the chance to clear my name that I'd thrown caution to the wind. I'd taken his offer to help me find out who really killed Heather in blind faith, and now I'd slept with him. Everything had spiraled out of control. Everything was wrong. Suddenly, the urge to pee came over me and was very aware of how tightly I was wrapped in a blanket.

"Um, Haywood, can you help unravel me? I really have to pee and can't do that wrapped up like a sausage."

"Oh, yes, of course. Here, I'll untuck it, and then I'll leave you to … take care of that and then we can talk. If you are up for it."

I nodded. Haywood walked me away from the fire of the living room and toward the bathroom. I was still a bit disoriented and was happy to have a steadying arm. As the door to the bathroom shut, I turned to the mirror and stared at my reflection while willing myself to be strong. I had to face it now. Alison was dead. Heather was dead. And I was a fugitive. Was Haywood an … accomplice? Lover? Friend? Would he lose his job?

I took a deep breath, wrapped a large white towel around my body, and picked up the blanket that Haywood had dressed me in. Breathe in slowly, breathe out slowly. Breathe in slowly, breathe out slowly. Big deep breath in and then blow it out. Calm. I steadied myself. "Okay, Clarke," I said to the mirror, "let's go get some fucking answers."

CHAPTER 13

Haywood

I sat in the living room by the fire, trying to compose myself. She would come out here any minute, and I would have to explain. She'd heard that the police department was looking for her, and I wasn't sure if she had time to connect the dots yet. Why would the police department not know where she was if she was in my custody? Why indeed? What a mess. I did not do messes.

My sovereign had bound my ability to tell Clarke everything, but I had to give her something. After last night, it pained me to lie to her. I shouldn't even have let last night happen. I knew better. She was vulnerable. I should have been strong enough to resist the attraction. This pull toward her was getting out of hand.

I'd known Clarke for so many years, had witnessed her heartbreak and loneliness, but had never spoken with her, never really known her, never been able to touch her directly, only influence elements in her orbit. I'd been caught off guard by the reality of her, intoxicated by her proximity. And then she'd reached for me and looked at me with those desperately sad eyes, and I … I'd complicated everything. I did not make mistakes.

As much as I tried, I could not deny my feelings for her now. My heart stopped when I woke to find the entire bedroom encased in ice. Clarke was pale blue and unresponsive, but much to my relief, still alive. She did not remember or realize what she'd done in the car and was asleep the second time, but there would be no avoiding telling her the truth once she knowingly experienced her powers. I had not lied to her; it had snowed last night, and the heater had broken—because she lowered the temperature in the cabin so fast it could not keep up. Everything was out of control. Everything was … wrong.

The news of Alison's death was most alarming. It made what I had to do much more difficult. I needed time. I needed her thinking clearly and rationally. I needed her ….

No, no more of this. I would compose myself and do what I came here to do. My feelings were inconsequential. The fate of Teleran was at stake. Teleran, my home, was faced with death and decimation. We did not know why, but about thirty years ago, our realm had started declining gently. It had happened slowly at first, but things had escalated a few months ago.

Teleran was bleeding into Earth and vice versa. If things got any worse, my world would be gone forever. It would fuse with Earth, exposing and likely killing my people.

Teleran had become our new home millions of years ago when Earth became uninhabitable to us. Legends say that we—the Estival and Obscurus, or collectively, the fae—lived in harmony and prosperity in the early days on Earth. Magical creatures like the *dosiuranus* were our protectors and friends until the fated day of the collision with the *Furrem Mirots*, a six-mile-wide asteroid. Its impact killed half the Earth's population in seconds and decimated the terrain.

Many more died as the air was poisoned. The asteroid contained an element that weakened us—iron—which had been aerosolized by the impact. With our accelerated healing, we could have adapted to a new atmosphere, but the true devastation was the ash and darkness that blanketed the Earth. The heavy layers of burning ash and lack of sunlight caused mass deterioration of the vegetation, thus removing our food source. At the time, all fae were what humans refer to as vegans. It would have been unthinkable to eat our friends, the animals. Many of them also perished as their food chain collapsed. We were sick and starving. There was a choice to make.

The remaining fae, those with the most strength, came together and joined their magic to create a pocket realm where we could live and thrive, retaining our magic and near-eternal vitality. No one alive now remembers how this was done save the Alternae, our elders, and possibly our sovereigns. Our life cycles were long but not infinite; our souls would recycle during our rebirth gifting us the closest thing to eternal life that existed. At three hundred and five, I was considered young by fae standards. My magic, like all the fae, manifested during my thirtieth year. I had all the normal fae traits, speed, the ability to control weak-minded individuals with minor manipulations, and heightened sense of all five senses coupled with the powers of the light fae, water and air magic with the ability to manipulate both. I was thankful for my magic and thankful for the haven of Teleran where I could use them. On Earth, I could use my magical abilities, but it was like having a blanket thrown over them. I had limits and felt depleted if I used them to access. I could only remain on Earth in short bursts of time and would have to return to Teleran to recharge.

Some said the fae who remained on Earth after the rest moved to Teleran forfeited their magic and became mortal, thus creating the first humans. I couldn't imagine ever making that decision by choice. It was widely known to all fae, however, that some fae had retreated to the deepest fathoms of the sea, and some had shifted into the animals that serve as cultivators of life, maintaining the Earth's fragile ecosystem, such as bees, bats, and butterflies.

There was an ancient prophecy that instructed in veiled terms how to save Teleran, but no one seemed to remember anything else about it. The scroll on which the prophecy was written was lost long ago. Rulers from both the Estival and Obscurus had sought wisdom from our elders, the Alternae, to no avail.

When Solana, my sovereign and ruler of the Estival, asked me to watch over Clarke—a fae born in the human world—as her protector. I was intrigued but didn't question my assignment. This practice wasn't common as far as I knew, but I did as I was instructed.

A few weeks ago, I was tasked with retrieving Clarke personally since she was already under my care. Solana led me to believe that new intel had presented itself and that we needed to bring all the fae that remained in the human world to Teleran. She said she believed this would bolster our strength.

After spending more time with Clarke, I had a growing suspicious that Solana had deceived me. We didn't need everyone; we just needed Clarke. Somehow, she was the key to reversing our fate. Her powers had begun to awaken when she entered her thirtieth year. I did not know that our salvation could be in the human world or with her—only that I'd been charged with her safety since shortly after her birth. Solana had made it so I was only able to help her in times of great distress, so I would be drawn to her when she was in extreme physical pain or emotional intensity.

I had never revealed myself to her before—could not even if I had wanted to. Until her powers emerged, I was invisible to her. It baffled me when she saw me in her prison cell. I was so used to her not seeing me. I should have taken her home to Teleran immediately. I made a mistake. My curiosity had gotten the better of me. I was meant to take her then, but she drew me in. I felt compassion toward her. How could I tell this already broken girl that she wasn't even human? That she was fae, an Estival, or light-sided fae, specifically. She knew nothing of our world. I had a notion of gaining her trust first and then finding a way to tell her the truth. Maybe if she heard why we needed her, she'd come willingly. Maybe she still would.

I had lied to her though. I wasn't a human detective. I was an emissary, a diplomat, and a nobleman. I had planted my colleague, Luck, at the police station to help get her out of prison shortly after I realized our kind was now corporal to her. I thought if I could help Clarke clear her name and find out who killed her roommate, she would have cause to trust me. My plan had failed. Someone was clearly targeting her, killing her roommate and now her best friend. I had sensed as much, and that's why I went back to her apartment to see if I could sense something that was missing in the case files I had stolen. I had found the murder weapon lodged along with some old chewing gum behind the trash receptacle in the alley behind her condo. Luck was to come to retrieve it, so it could be entered into evidence.

Clarke was being targeted, but how and why? Did this person want Clarke dead as well? She could be in grave danger.

When I learned of Alison going missing, I admit that I had panicked. I was worried about Clarke's safety. I had to get her somewhere safe and then tell her the truth. Now Alison was dead. I had a terrible feeling that everything was escalating. I had run out of time.

To make matters worse, her powers were leaking out of her like a sieve. There was no more time to break this to her gently, which was another reason for the remote location of the cabin. I had no way to know what her reaction would be. She could detonate. I did not know what she was capable of, and for the first time, I felt true fear. Clarke was volatile, with powers that were unparalleled in all of Teleran; not even my sovereign was so powerful. The signature essence of Clarke's power weirdly reminded me of another powerful fae I knew, an Obscurus or dark fae, but it had to be a fluke. It would be impossible for Clarke to have any ties to *her*.

I had to stall. I had to give her just enough truth. Just enough to calm her. As the bathroom door creaked open, I steeled myself to meet her gaze as her determined, bright-green eyes met mine. Eyes that reminded me of the first time I'd seen them.

That first time I'd felt a pull to her, she'd been crying in the corner of her closet, holding a pillow to muffle her cries, clutching it like it was a lifeline. She was far too young to feel such heartbreak, but there was nothing I could do. I'd never seen such sadness. So I sat next to her in her closet until her cries quieted and her breathing became rhythmic. She'd fallen asleep in her hideaway. I could hear raised voices coming from the floor below me, but that wasn't my concern. I decided I'd done what I came there to do. The child was safe, her health wasn't in danger, and her heart would heal. She had not suffered a mortal wound.

The second time, she was laughing and swimming with friends in the ocean. Her joy was such a contrast to the last time I'd seen her that it took me by surprise. She stayed out all day in that ocean having the time of her life. Then she looked around and realized she was alone; her friends had gone back up to the beach, leaving her. She had strayed a bit too far from the shore and began swimming in. I saw and felt the moment she panicked, realizing she was too tired to beat the powerful undercurrent. It pulled her farther out to sea as if something had hold of her leg and was dragging her out and down. She sank beneath the waves. I took a breath and plunged in after her. Letting a bit of my power out, I tapped into my water magic to guide the current to move her up and toward the beach, just enough to carry her to shore but not enough that she would feel my influence. When she made it to the sandy beach, she collapsed, exhausted but okay.

The third time was different. I felt her tug so hard that I was shocked she didn't end up falling straight into Teleran, ripping a portal open with her will. Her craving for power, the power that surely lay dormant inside of her, was staggering. She was a little older and dressed in all black. Her skin was ghostly pale, her body too skinny, but her mood was excited. She was chanting some human witch nonsense with a group of girls who were all dressed like her. I heard her wish and plea for a sign. What was the harm in indulging her? I sent a swirl of leaves dancing around her group of young ladies. The glee lit her face as she jumped up and looked around her. She loved it. She thought maybe her chant caused this. I found that I really enjoyed making her smile.

A few hours later, I felt her panic and fear. I arrived to see another female her age close to her face, saying some angry words to her. Clarke was scared and angry, livid really. She tugged again, searching for that power, the well inside her. I didn't like the attention she was gathering from the other children. Some were calling her things that were unacceptable. I decided to help her again and sent a swarm of bees to separate her from the girl closest to her, who then ran away screaming. The bees were entirely under my control. I didn't allow the bees to sting the girl … much. I just wanted her to leave Clarke alone.

Our next encounter happened when she was older, almost fully grown. I felt her fear, panic, and anger all at once. She was standing on a balcony in the rain, screaming with her arms outstretched toward two figures who were falling off the side of the balcony. I quickly sent a wave of my power to break their fall. Clearly, an incident had occurred. I seemed to be drawn to her in moments when she was getting into some sort of trouble. Her cohorts landed safely on the ground but not entirely unscathed. I heard a pop and a crack and winced. Clarke screamed again and ran inside. A moment later, she ran out from the building to where the two people lay. She seemed to have the situation under control, so I left her to her own devices.

After her mother passed, I sat as close to her as I could and watched her sob. She couldn't feel me, of course, but I placed my hand over hers. I felt like I needed to be there for her. I'd not seen her cry this much since she was a child, and I realized I hated the sight. I knew her mother was important to her, and for Clarke to grieve her so fiercely, she must have been a wonderful person. I held her until she quieted and slept. I lingered a few moments past that and watched her rest.

The most recent time I'd come to her, before all this murder business started, was on her thirtieth birthday. She was lovely in a black dress that hugged her hips, paired with red heels that sparkled when she moved. Her power was pulsing around her, but she didn't seem to notice. It bewitched me and everyone else around her. All were drawn to her like a moth to a flame. She was radiant. I couldn't tear my eyes from her smile, the contours of her mouth. To have known her all this time and not really seen her in all her glory until now—her light had been hidden, dimmed by the mortality she thought was her own. Something drew my attention back to Teleran at that moment, so I had to walk away from her, but I noticed that I really would rather have stayed.

I'd been pulled to her again a short few months later, which had never happened before, her moments of need usually spaced years apart. Her fear enveloped me so thoroughly that I felt like I was drowning. She was in a darkened room when I appeared to her, though my fae eyes could see the room clearly. Someone was lying dead on the bed in front of her. She was standing frozen, murmuring to herself, and clutching a phone in one hand and a flashlight in the other. Had she killed the human on the bed? Nothing about her indicated an ability to do such a thing, but having observed her only in brief moments of her life, I wasn't quite sure.

I blinked, and we were outside on the sidewalk by her condo building. She still seemed incoherent. I could hear the people around me talking about a murder investigation. Through the cracks of Clarke's shock, I sensed a deep sadness. She couldn't have murdered the girl in the bed; I felt guilty for even considering she could. I sat beside her on the sidewalk until a police officer ushered her toward a car with flashing blue lights.

When I appeared to Clarke next, she was in a prison cell. I sparked up a joint of marijuana (one of my only vices from the human world) and watched her. She seemed to startle and looked directly at where I was sitting in the cell next to hers. She'd never seen me before, had never even acted like she detected a presence near her. But then she called out once and then twice. She could see me. I'd known that as her powers developed, this was possible, but I'd still been shocked. After thirty years of being her guardian, her protector, I would finally get a chance to talk to her.

I broke out of my reverie of our past encounters in time to see she was standing in front of me—staring.

CHAPTER 14

Clarke

When I walked out of the bathroom, Haywood was staring at the fire in the hearth, lost in thought. I cleared my throat, alerting him of my presence, he looked up at me with a small smile.

"Clarke, I know we need to talk," Haywood said. "Let me know what questions you may have, and I'll try to answer them for you."

"I agree. Um, let me just grab some clothes first," I said, clutching the knot in my towel like a vise.

"Wait! Let me—" Haywood's voice sounded panicked as he rose from his seat near the fire and tried to launch himself in front of me as I reached for the bedroom door and turned the knob.

"What the—?" I stammered as I took in the room's appearance. It looked like a tidal wave had come through and drenched everything.

"*Cremtnux*, yeah, I was going to explain that first," he said.

"Cremma what? Is the roof leaking?"

"Um, never mind. Well, I … um … yes, there must be a hole in the roof somewhere."

My heart fluttered. Haywood always spoke with surety; he didn't stutter. The only time I'd ever seen him flustered was in our exodus out of town after he'd learned that Alison was missing. I winced at the thought.

All of my clothes, Alison's clothes, were in a bag on the floor, likely soaked from the inch of water that had collected there.

Haywood ushered me out of the doorway of the bedroom and closed the door.

"Let's sit."

"Okay …." Our bare feet left wet footprints on the hardwood floor as I let him lead me to the two chairs in front of the fire. I was still dressed only in the towel. He seemed to take note of that and grabbed the blanket from my arms and tucked it around my body. I was warmer sitting by the fire, all wrapped up, but nothing about this situation made me comfortable.

"Would you prefer I answer your questions first or …?" He trailed off, seeming not to know what to say.

"How about we start with what happened when you went to my condo?"

"Yes, of course, yes. The road to your place was all but blocked by several cars and media vans. I proceeded to park and assess the situation. As I drew closer to your place, I overheard a reporter saying that Alison was missing and that 'the suspect' had been missing ever since Alison's disappearance. They gave your name and description and gave a warning for people to be on the lookout for you, that they should call the authorities if anyone saw you or knew of your whereabouts. There is a reward to whomever supplies this information. You are suspected to be armed and dangerous …."

I hadn't realized my mouth was stuck hanging open until Haywood stopped recounting the horrors that were my life. One thing about his story stood out. I wasn't missing.

Until yesterday, the "authorities" knew exactly where I was—with Haywood.

"Why the hell did they say I was missing? The police department placed me with you. They know exactly where I've been."

Haywood expression shifted in a way that made me cringe. His hands were clasped in his lap, and his knuckles were turning white. Beads of sweat dotted his brow. He looked like he wanted to either throw up or bolt from the room. I watched him take a deep breath, school his features, and face me with determined eyes.

"That is one of the things I wanted to discuss with you."

A wave of dread hit me as my heart rate picked up.

"What the fuck do you mean that is one of the things you wanted to discuss with me?" I said pointedly as my eyes narrowed into slits.

"Um …," he stammered, "Clarke, I … I am so sorry. It was not my intention to deceive you. Well, temporarily, maybe." His eyes went wide, and his eyebrows shot up to the ceiling. "I'm not exactly working with the police department. I didn't lie when I said I was assigned to your case. Technically, I was. I know nothing I'm saying is making sense, but if you would just allow me a moment, I want to be as honest as I can be. Clarke, sit back down; what are you ...?"

I realized I was standing now, clutching my hands at my sides so hard I could feel my nails breaking the skin of my palms. He'd lied to me. Who the fuck was this guy? Rage had welled up inside me, and apparently, my body was readying itself for a brawl. He wasn't a detective? What the fuck was going on? Haywood's eyes went from trepidation to stunned to fear in one blink. The fire in the hearth flared as if mimicking my mood. I felt the bite of chill on my body then. When I'd jumped up, my towel had fallen. I was standing bare and angry. I quickly bent down, snatched up the towel, and sat down, wrapping the blanket back around myself and taking a deep breath. Breathe in slowly, breathe out slowly. Breathe in slowly, breathe out slowly. Big deep breath in and blow it—fuck it. I couldn't calm my wildly beating heart. With a force of sheer will, I replied calmly. I was determined to get the answers I needed from him.

"I will let you explain yourself, Hay—is Haywood even your name?!" I reined my anger back in. "Oh my— seriously, I'm about to lose my shit"—I drew in a deep breath—"but I know you risked a lot to try to help me. And since you've helped me, I am going to try to give you the benefit of the doubt," I said through halfway-gritted teeth.

"Yes, of course. As I said, I was sent to help with your case in a roundabout way. I'm not here to hurt you, Clarke; you must know that. The media thinks you are missing because you technically are. I am not a detective with the Charlotte police department."

"What the fuck does that mean, Haywood? Who sent you then? Who the fuck are you?" Oh my fucking—I'd slept with this man. Did he fucking kidnap me? Fuck. Fuck. Fuck.

"Let's say I'm a third-party freelance investigator," he said as he interrupted my freak out.

Okay, that sounded like a thing, right? I had to hear him out. If he had a reasonable explanation, then fine. If he didn't, also fine. Well, not fine, but I'd act fine just long enough to get the fuck out of here. If he'd manipulated and abducted me, what were his motives? He couldn't be the murderer, right? Could he be the fucking murderer? Was he playing with my head, and just when I least expected it, *bam*, I would be dead too? Oh, fuck, fuckity, fuck. Okay, Clarke, play it cool. He's been kind. That couldn't have been faked, could it?

My past relationship dramas suggested otherwise. People are way capable of hiding their true selves, lying in wait until the perfect opportunity to fuck you over. Well, Haywood was in for a rude awakening. Life had trained me for psychological warfare by giving me a father who would mentally abuse me on a daily basis. I was just off my game. Losing your friends, family, and freedom will do that to a girl. Time to buck up and put my big girl panties back on. Unfortunately, they'd have to be metaphorical panties since my real ones—well, Alison's—were soaked through in my bag in the bedroom. Regardless, we got this, self. We so got this.

"Let's say you are," I replied with a steely calm.

"I can honestly say that is exactly what I am," he said seriously.

"But you can't tell me specifically who you work for?"

"I'm not presently at liberty to say. Even if I was, it would not make sense. But soon. I can tell you everything soon," he said while sounding like he was reassuring himself more than he was reassuring me.

"I guess I really have no other choice but to trust you then."

"Clarke, I—"

"No, you hold all the cards here, Haywood. I'm a fugitive. I have no one. I'm alone in this world, and right now, you are the only thing standing between me and prison. And I really don't want to go back there. But come on, you have to give me something. Anything." My voice cracked. Shit, was I pleading? My fear and hope were bleeding together. It was all I could do not to implode. I was feeling too much. My veins were blazing with an energy I'd never felt before. It was probably terror. That or this is what happens when you literally hold in a monster panic attack because you're not sure if you just fucked a psychopath.

"Yes, I can try for you," he replied gently. Like really gently. So gently that my resolve fractured. Maybe he was telling the truth.

"Officer Luck is working for me."

"Uh, what?" Shocked. I wasn't expecting that.

"That's how I was able to remove your tracking device and avoid immediate action from the authorities. I had her run interference, so they would think you never left Alison's."

"So Officer Luck works for you and whoever you work for?"

"Yes."

"So that's why no one has come after me until they reported Alison missing?"

"Correct."

"That makes … sense actually." And it did. Sort of. He could still be nuts, and he could still chop me up in small bits and spread me up and down the Blue Ridge Parkway, which I assumed we were close to. He'd said we were in the mountains, right?

"When I went to your condo to see if I could find anything the authorities missed, I was able to go in through the back entrance. I found evidence of four people in the room in which Heather was murdered. You, Heather, Alison, and an unidentified male. I also found this." He held up a clear plastic bag containing a wicked-looking knife. It had a sharp blade with deep serrations and a wooden handle with a dark stain all over it, and … was that gum?

"The handle is covered in blood, Clarke. Heather's blood. It was hidden in the alleyway of your condo complex behind a dumpster. The gum on the side held it between the wall and the trash receptacle."

I was more than a little shocked. Haywood had found the murder weapon. Or he was the killer, and then, of course, he'd have the murder weapon. But if my prints weren't on it, it could be proof of my innocence. This could be my chance to clear my name.

I'd never seen the knife before. It looked like some special kind, not something you used in the kitchen. Assuming my prints couldn't possibly be on it, I felt relief. Then my mind started running back through everything Haywood had said.

"Okay, while this is an amazing find and could potentially clear my name, and I am grateful, what evidence? An unidentified male? I'm pretty sure no 'males' have ever been to our condo, at least not in the year I've been living there. Heather didn't date or have a boyfriend, and I never brought anyone home."

"Interesting."

I narrowed my eyes. Was he making a joke about my love life right now? Really? Whatever, Clarke, focus.

"That's weird right?"

"Yes, Clarke." He paused. "Do you know anyone who has any reason to cause you or your friends harm?"

"No! No, not at all. … Well, I don't know." Do you want to hurt me? Did you hurt my friends? I almost asked but stopped myself. "We have to go to the police. This evidence, it could have prints on it. If this guy's prints are on the murder weapon …," I trailed off.

"I agree."

"Huh? You do?"

"I've already contacted Luck, and she is supposed to come by to collect the weapon. She'll somehow make it look like the police found it, so the evidence goes through the proper channels and remains admissible in court. Your name could indeed be cleared, and that would help things become less … complicated."

"This is good, Haywood. Thank you, truly, for going there and trying to get me out of this mess, for keeping me safe. You don't even really know me, and it means a lot that you would go to all this trouble to help me." Even if I didn't trust him, I was thankful. That much was true. I laid it on a little thick with that part about keeping me safe. If he was planning to murder me, maybe he'd feel guilty about it now and change his mind.

"Of course, Clarke. You are more than welcome."

Knock. Knock.

"That should be Luck now," he said as he got up from his chair and walked toward the door. Haywood cracked the door open and quickly exchanged the knife and a bundle of things with Officer Luck. He closed the door and returned.

"I asked Luck to bring you some clothes since yours are likely soaked. We can get yours dried, but she brought you some things to change into."

"That was thoughtful. Thank you. Why didn't she come in? We go way back, you know."

"Yes," he said with a warm smile, "I know. I'm sure she would have loved nothing more than to get to know you, but she had to return so as not to rouse suspicion."

"Oh, yes, that makes sense." I paused. "So what now?"

"We wait."

"We just wait."

"Yes, I'm hoping that with this additional evidence, your name will be cleared. Then we figure out what happens next."

"Or they'll find my prints on it, and then I'm public enemy number one again."

"Clarke, I really don't think—"

"It's alright, Haywood; I was only half joking."

"Oh."

"I think I'm going to go change now," I said, needing some space from him and not to be naked anymore. We'd blurred the lines last night. It was a mistake. A mistake I wouldn't be making again.

"Yes, that is a splendid idea."

It seemed he agreed then. Good. On that fact, we were aligned. We'd gotten caught up in the situation. That's all. Nothing else was going on here. I'd needed an escape, and he was willing: end of story.

"But don't think this conversation is over," I said. "I still don't understand most of what you said. I still need answers."

"Yes, I know."

A memory of Alison and my thirtieth birthday party suddenly came out of nowhere. She'd planned the whole thing, telling me to dress hot and meet at her place before heading down to the sushi restaurant that took up most of the bottom level of her building. It was more like a club than a restaurant, although they actually had really good food. The owner was a trip though. She pranced around in a glittery cowboy hat, pouring shots for willing and unwilling patrons alike.

As I stepped into the elevator at Alison's place, I punched in her apartment floor number and sighed as the doors closed. I'd been so excited to celebrate with my friends, but also felt a little overwhelmed. I didn't like to be the center of attention, and knowing Alison, I'd be thrust right into the center.

The apartment building where Alison lived was popularly known as "the pink building" because the outer walls were all pink glass. It was quite the sight, towering over the buildings around it. Pink was fitting for her because she also decorated most of her apartment in that color. I'd found out recently that her building was never supposed to be pink; the builders had ordered the wrong color glazing. Once it was up though, it would've been too much of a hassle to take them down and redo them. The building became iconic, so in the end, it was a happy accident.

The elevator dinged, alerting me that it was time to exit. I rounded the hallway until I arrived at Alison's door. I could hear music thumping loudly from inside. I texted her instead of knocking, knowing she wouldn't hear me over the noise.

The door swung open, and I was pulled into a tight hug.

"Oh my god, girl! Let's get this party started!" she yelled as the champagne in her glass dribbled on the floor.

I stepped back and beamed. Alison was in a pink body-hugging dress with heels that made her almost a foot taller than me. She was holding two champagne glasses and shoved the one without lipstick stains on it toward me.

"You look so hot!" she continued. "I have a surprise for you!"

"Where is everybody?!" I questioned, surveying her empty apartment. Our friends were supposed to be joining us, but maybe they were running late.

"Oh, girl, they are already downstairs getting everything ready for us," she said, turning the music down so we didn't have to shout.

"Oh, cool! Well, I'm ready except for my shoes." I gestured to my red chucks. I had chosen to wear a tight little black dress that came to mid-thigh. I actually liked the contrast of my fancy dress with my casual shoes but knew Alison would never let me out like this. She had a closet full of towering heels and had already said I could borrow some of hers.

"Oh, yes, girl, come into the kitchen; your birthday present is on the bar." She pointed to a pink and white striped box with a giant pink bow on top.

"Alison, thank you! You didn't have to get me anything." I protested politely but secretly was so excited. Alison gave the best gifts, and I couldn't wait to see what she'd come up with.

"Uh, duh, Clarke, it's your thirtieth birthday. I wouldn't not get you something, silly. I know when I turn thirty next year, you'll spoil the shit out of me too."

I smiled at that. We were only a year a part, but Alison was already joking about how she was turning into an old woman. She would always complain about her fine lines that were non-existent since she got Botox regularly or the way her knees ached after a long day at the salon. I never brought up the fact that as I got closer to turning thirty, I'd felt more energized than ever, and there wasn't a wrinkle in sight on my face even though I hadn't journeyed down the path of injectables. I was a happier person all around and felt like that was why I was always buzzing with energy. Plus, my mom had always looked amazing for her age and was thankful to have her genetics on my side. Alison liked to bring it up though. She would often say things like, "Why do you have to be so fucking pretty, Clarke?" or "I hate you and your perfect skin." She'd always laugh, and I'd join her. She talked to everyone like that, and it seemed to me that that was how she gave compliments.

I approached the box and tore open the wrapping. Lifting the lid off while noting the insignia embossed on top, I was stunned. "You didn't," I said breathlessly.

"I did!" She beamed.

I took out the shoe bag inside the box and held it. From the insignia on the outside of the box to the shoe bag, I knew exactly what lay inside. I carefully pulled out the most beautiful glossy red heels I'd ever seen, complete with the iconic red soles. My eyes blurred as I looked up at Alison to thank her. She was grinning like a little kid at Christmas.

"Do you like them?" She asked knowingly.

"Of course, I like them! I love them, Alison, but they're too much! You shouldn't have spent this much on me."

"Whew, your face made me think you didn't like them at first, and I was just going to take them back since we are the same size. But, girl, no, I wanted you to love them, and they are birthday shoes. Everyone gets shoes on their birthday, duh. And they'll look amazing with your outfit tonight. Maybe you'll even snag a boyfriend tonight or just, ya know, a tonight boyfriend," she said with a wink while waggling her brows at me suggestively.

"Thank you so much. I don't even know what to say."

"Say you'll put them on and get your ass in gear. Everyone's waiting, and I'm ready to get my drink on."

"You're already drinking," I said with a chuckle, pointing to her champagne.

"Uh, girl, you know what I mean."

"I do." I smiled and went to sit on her couch. I took off my shoes and put on the new ones that I knew for a fact cost more than my monthly mortgage payment.

The shoes glided on and felt like heaven. I stood up and earned a whoop from Alison.

"Now, that's a hot outfit!" She boomed as she looped her arm through mine and guided me out the door. "Let's go celebrate, Clarke!"

"Let's," I'd agreed as I'd smiled back at her.

The memory of when Alison had gifted me those damn shoes broke my heart. It kicked off one of the best nights of my life, except when Cody had been way too drunk and got a bit grabby toward the end of the night.

I'd loved those shoes so much when she gave them to me, and now … now that my world was crumbling, I wished she never had. They were now being used as evidence against me. I missed her, and I was confused and broken. I turned away from Haywood in a daze and went to get dressed, shrugging off the chilling memory that had invaded. I needed to focus. Later. Later, I could relive all the memories of my best friend and let myself crumble with them.

CHAPTER 15

I walked away from Haywood, clutching the clothes Officer Luck had brought close to my chest. No, not Officer Luck. Just Luck then? I guess it didn't matter either way.

I changed in the second bedroom of the cabin since the one Haywood and I had shared was now flooded thanks to the roof leak. I shut the door behind me and slid down it. My bare ass hit the worn-in rug.

"I can do this," I whispered to myself. Saying it out loud didn't make it any more believable. My life had become such a big fucked-up mess. Ugh, I didn't have time for this wallowing. "Pull yourself together, Clarke," I said a little louder. With renewed resolve, I pushed myself up to get dressed.

A terrible gurgling sound came from my stomach, reminding me that I hadn't eaten since yesterday before Haywood barged in and ushered me here. I had come up with a plan. I supposed eating something and keeping my strength up should be part of that plan.

I pulled out a pair of gray drawstring pants and a plain, oversized white T-shirt. Luck had even included some granny panties and a white sports bra. I looked a bit like a little kid wearing their dad's clothes but was happy to be dry and covered.

"So are we eating while we wait, or did we not get provisions in our hasty exodus out of town?" I asked as I returned to the living room.

"Certainly, we most definitely can eat," he replied, sounding relieved.

Relieved that I wasn't asking more questions, or relieved because he could kill me easier by poisoning my food? Shit, I had to stop. He could be telling me the truth. He could—whatever. We had to wait anyway. If my plan was comprised of me escaping my potential kidnapper and murderer, I couldn't just go traipsing off while the actual cops were after me. I had to hope that Luck came through and that someone else's prints were found on the murder weapon. If that happened, then I'd steal Haywood's car and get the hell out of here. I could swing by my condo and grab the necessities and my mom's necklace and then keep fucking driving. I had a stash of cash hidden under my bed that I'd been saving for a rainy day. I could get away from all of this and start a new life far away from all the death and this man who was definitely keeping something from me. Could I really take the chance that it was a harmless lie?

Even if he didn't kidnap me, even if he wasn't a crazy murderer, I couldn't stay with him. I made my mind up. I'd buy my time until word came back from Luck, and then I'd get the fuck out.

CHAPTER 16

Haywood

Clarke was taking the few truths I had shared with her remarkably well. Finding the murder weapon had worked in my favor. I could feel her panic settle, and trust was back in her eyes. We ate in companionable silence. Clarke had not resumed her questioning. I had bought time. She still thought she was a human. Her powers seemed to have calmed with her mood.

I knew her prints could not be on that knife. As soon as Luck got back, she would enter it into evidence, and Clarke's name would be cleared. Then I could tell her everything. She would trust me then.

Everything would be right.

When we finished eating, Clarke excused herself to the bedroom, saying she was exhausted. I let her walk away from me as an unfamiliar feeling took root. Longing. I had to let her go. Nothing good could come from pursuing anything with her. I'd already made a mess of my mission. I could not continue to stray in my resolve. I found that I, too, was exhausted, so I tucked myself into the small couch in the living room. I would greet tomorrow as the professional I was and get Clarke's name cleared and freedom secured. Then I could tell her everything and hope she would agree to come with me to Teleran.

CHAPTER 17

Clarke

Beautiful and amazing creatures surrounded me in a field full of sunflowers and lavender. The creatures were people but not quite. Some had masks fashioned with huge petals, and some had complexions that looked like the night sky and hair full of stars and whorls of misty galaxies. I continued to survey this amazing place where I'd woken up. Two beings approached me timidly. Gold flakes highlighted their cheekbones, and they wore identical jewelry that made the points of their ears more pronounced. I suddenly realized what I was looking at—the fae, the ones I'd adored reading about over and over. I loved devouring world after world, often escaping for hours to places that were unbound by the restraints of reality. These fae were more exquisite than any I'd ever conjured in my head or any that had been painted by the words of authors I adored. They were delicate but strong. They circled around me, investigating curiously. One reached out to me, and I extended my hand in return. Right as our palms started to collide, I heard a familiar voice call my name.

"Clarke?"

I stirred from my sleep as a warm hand gently stroked my cheek. Ugh, it was Haywood. Why did I have to like him touching me so much? Fuck him.

"I'm up," I said, sounding grouchier than I intended. I was not a morning person.

"I thought we could wait for Luck's call together. She said she'd be contacting me shortly."

Oh, hell yes. That got me moving.

"I took the liberty of washing and drying your clothes from your bag. I've folded them as well." He gestured to a stack on the dresser in the second bedroom I'd slept in. Alone. Haywood had slept on the small couch in the living room.

"Thank you so much." Why did he have to be so nice? His kindness and helpfulness made it so hard to remember that I could not trust him.

I inhaled and smelled fresh coffee brewing. And he made coffee. Seriously, this dude. With each display of kindness, my resolve was cracking.

We walked together to the kitchen and sat across from each other at the small table. The same table where he'd cleaned my bloody face … where I'd grabbed him and we … and—stop it, Clarke! I could feel my cheeks heat. Great. My body didn't care that we couldn't trust him. Nope, that treacherous bitch would've asked him to kiss her again. Body parts spasmed as a very vivid flashback entered my mind. Fuck. He seemed unfazed by the same memories as his face remained neutral. Good. That's exactly what I want from him—nothing. Right. The tinge of hurt I felt must be indigestion from the coffee I'd guzzled down.

Buzz … buzz. Haywood's phone vibrated and lit up on the table. He pressed the speaker phone option and answered Luck's call.

"Luck, Clarke and I are here. What is your update?"

"You were right, sir. Clarke's prints were nowhere on the murder weapon."

I let out a breath that I'd been holding as soon as Luck's name flashed on Haywood's phone screen. An embarrassed sob of relief escaped my lips, and Haywood reached over and put his hand over mine. I jerked back and looked up at him. A pained expression crossed his face as he furrowed his brows. I took his hand in mine to try to cover up the fact that I'd actually recoiled from his touch. I squeezed his hand and smiled, and he squeezed and smiled back. Play it cool, Clarke.

"That is splendid news, Luck. Were you able to determine whose prints were on the weapon?"

"We were, sir. It's Cody Mason. Alison Villareal's boyfriend."

What—the—fuck? Cody? He killed Heather? Did that mean he killed Alison? Wait, how did Cody even know Heather? They'd never met, as far as I knew.

"Officers are being dispatched as we speak to detain him. It is likely that Clarke will be cleared of the murder charge in the Heather Dunn case."

"Were they able to get any DNA off of the gum stuck to the side of the handle?" Haywood pressed.

"No, sir. DNA came back inconclusive."

"What about the shoe prints?" I interrupted.

"Your lack of an alibi and those shoe prints are the extent of the evidence against you, but I advise you not to leave the state. You will still be a person of interest in her case, but I'm confident they will drop all charges when we get a full confession from Mason," Luck replied.

"So now what? What about Alison? Do you have evidence that Cody killed her too?"

"Nothing yet, but we are still processing her body. The autopsy is scheduled for today."

"So am I still a person of interest in her disappearance and death?"

"You are but not for long. I'm sure of it. The chatter around the station suggests that because he is Alison's boyfriend, he has a motive for her disappearance at the very least. His prints were on the murder weapon, which solidly ties him to Heather's murder, and they have reason to believe the murders are connected."

"How? Am I missing something?"

"You," Haywood interjected.

"What about me?"

"You are the connection."

"I don't understand. I thought you said—"

"Heather and Alison were the closest people to you. Heather was your roommate. Alison was your best friend. Was there a reason Cody would want you to suffer? A reason he would wish you harm?"

"I have no idea. Seriously, that is twisted, Haywood."

"Maybe, but it is what the police will ask you. You'll be brought in for questioning again. You'll have to explain to them why you ran—"

"I didn't run! You took me!" I said, sounding more irate than I meant to.

Haywood took a deep breath before he replied. "Yes, and there isn't a way to explain that to them. You must tell them you ran because you were scared, that you thought whoever was responsible was likely after you too. Tell them you didn't feel safe. Maintain your innocence. They will probably take pity on you."

"Haywood is correct, Clarke. This is the best course of action. Sir, if I may offer a suggestion?"

"Yes, Luck?"

"Clarke should call Officer Cain. She seemed to be fond of Clarke while she was here. Clarke, if you call her and explain to her what happened, or what Haywood suggests you say happened, I'm sure she will bring you in herself."

"I need a minute here, guys," I said. They were right. This sounded like a pretty good plan. And it would get me away from Haywood in the process. I could do this. If they believed me, then I could go home. I would be free. I had to do this. I could call Officer Cain. I liked her; she had been kind to me.

"What will happen to you if I do this?" I asked Haywood.

"I'll be fine. They do not know me. You'll be free."

"What about your … your third-party investigation or whatever? You know, the people who hired you."

"That is not your concern. Do this, clear your name, and go home. I will find you there."

"Oh, okay … um, sure," I replied, not knowing what else to say. I felt happy that I'd be seeing him again. What was wrong with me? I felt like I still wasn't getting the entire story from him. Seeing him again would give me the chance to get the whole story. If Cody was the killer, then Haywood really had been trying to help me all along. My heart throbbed at the thought. I cared far too much for this man than I should. Somehow, he held a little piece of me, and I wasn't sure how or when it'd happened. My head was screaming that he was still hiding something though. I could feel it. This time, my brain won the battle with my heart.

"Thank you, Luck, for everything, and I guess I'll be seeing you soon, right?"

"Yes, Clarke, I'll be at the police station when you get here."

"Cool. So how do I get in touch with Officer Cain?"

"I'll forward Haywood her personal cell. You may call her when you are ready."

"Thanks again."

We sat in silence for a full minute before either of us spoke. He got up and turned on the TV in the living room just as breaking news of Cody's arrest came across.

"So I guess I can call Officer Cain now," I said, breaking the pause. I jumped up from my seat at the table.

"Of course," he said as he handed me his phone. "I'll leave you to your privacy.

CHAPTER 18

I kicked a rock across the pavement as I waited for Officer Cain to pick me up. Haywood had dropped me off a half hour ago at a random gas station a few miles from the cabin. He didn't want Officer Cain to ask questions about whose cabin I'd been staying at; he thought she should pick me up in a neutral location. Our goodbyes were brief. There really wasn't a lot to say.

I was full of self-loathing. If Haywood's theory was correct, then Cody had killed both Alison and Heather to hurt me. I did not know why he would do that, but if that was true, then it was all my fault. All of it. Sure, Cody had made some unwanted advances my way when he was drinking, but how the fuck was that related to him wanting to destroy my life and kill the people closest to me? It just didn't make sense.

I looked up at the sound of a car pulling into the gas station, tires crunching through the ice and sludge. It pulled up close to where I was, and I recognized the driver. Officer Cain put the car in park and exited the vehicle. She walked over and pulled me in for a hug. What the—?

"I'm so glad you are okay. I'm so glad you called me. I knew when I met you that you couldn't have killed your roommate. I've been doing this for a long time, and I know the look of a killer. You didn't have it."

I backed out of her embrace. Her affection surprised me, but it was comforting to hear that she didn't think I was a killer.

"You must have been terrified," she continued.

"Uh, yeah, I was."

"I have to take you directly to the station for questioning. Cody Mason is in the interrogating room as we speak."

"Yes, of course, I'm ready. Did he confess? Do we know anything about Alison yet?"

"I drove straight here after you called me, so I'm not sure, but we will find out shortly. Oh, you poor thing," she said, rubbing my arm comfortingly. "Let's get you in the car. Maybe we can get you something to eat on the way to the station?"

"Sure, I would like that."

It took us an hour into our trip to find a place to grab food. The snow slowly faded away and turned to wet streets pooling with mud the farther we got from the mountains. Officer Cain pointed out how early in the season that snowstorm had been, apparently one of the earliest on record. I guess she was right; it was only early fall, but our weather in the South was always an anomaly. You could have freezing temperatures in the morning and then be sunbathing by the afternoon.

Shortly after stuffing my face with the greasy goodness that Officer Cain got for me from one of the fast-food places along the highway, we pulled up to the Charlotte-Mecklenburg Police Department. The vast building loomed before me like a bad omen.

Officer Cain covered my hand with hers as a show of comfort and solidarity.

"You ready, dear?" she asked.

I took a deep breath in and sighed. "Yep, I'm as ready as I'll ever be."

***

The moment my butt hit the cold metal of the chair in the interrogation room again, I panicked. I was here again. How was I back here? It'd only been a week but felt like it had been years. So much had changed since I sat here last. I had changed.

Would I ever leave this building again? What was going to happen to Cody? Did he kill Alison too? Did he really do this to hurt me somehow, like Haywood suggested?

Haywood.

I couldn't think about him right now. I couldn't think about how he'd tried to help me when I had no one. I couldn't think about the reason he would do that. I couldn't think about how it felt for his hands to—nope, not going there. I had to try to forget the time we spent together. All his confusing explanations. I just couldn't.

My brain was short-circuiting. I could barely remember the past week. My mind was a swirling vortex of questions and confusion, with one unbelievable occurrence after another.

A week ago, my biggest problem was finding a suitable exclusive fuck buddy. My most stressful obstacle was passing my next exam and finishing my bachelor's degree. My horizon had been full of possibilities. Finally, I'd been living the life I'd always wanted, a life I'd been proud of, a life my mom would've been proud of. I was ready to prove that losing her wouldn't define my future. I was so ready that I could taste it, see it, feel it.

That funk I was in a week ago had been a harbinger of what was to come. I'd thought it was just a phase, a blip-something I was only going to entertain for a few more days and then, bam, back to killing it at life.

Ha, killing it at life, huh? Well, death had certainly surrounded me. I was a shroud of death. I blanketed those closest to me and snuffed out their lives. It didn't matter that I hadn't been the one to murder them. I was still the cause, wasn't I? If it wasn't for me, Heather would be living her beautiful, quiet life, and Alison would still be living her vivacious one.

Whether I understood it or not, I was their common denominator. Once I entered their lives, their days were numbered. My mom, my dad, Heather, and Alison.

Anguish gripped my heart. The rhythmic beat of my life force choked and sputtered, and my vision started to darken. I brought my hands around my body as if to hold myself together, to stop myself from melting into a puddle on the floor. My hands gripped my biceps so tightly, their warmth seemed to defrost my hardened heart. They were so warm, so warm, so … hot!

"Fuck! Ouch," I said aloud to the empty room.

I looked down at my hands, still grasping myself in a hug. Small flames licked the edges of my fingers. I peeled my hands away from their hold and held them outstretched. I blinked. Just hands. No flames.

Whew. I'm really losing it. "Get it together, Clarke." I couldn't afford to lose it like I had the last time I was here. I had to get a grip. Last time, I'd almost not regained my sanity. Talking to myself and imagining apparitions was bad, but seeing flames shoot out of my fingertips, that was borderline certifiable. And being certifiably insane while being questioned by the police, again, would likely land me in a nice, long stay in a padded party room. Nope, not happening. "Shake yourself out of this, Clarke." We got this. I needed to be strong enough for Heather and Alison. If Cody did this, he needed to be brought to justice. I could do this for them. I had to.

Steely determination filled me. I lengthened my spine and started nice, long, even breaths right as the door swung open.

Luck barreled through.

"Clarke," she said urgently and then paused. She glanced around the room and seemed to take note of the camera pointed in our direction.

"Miss Carpenter," she corrected, "they are just finishing interrogating Mr. Mason now and should be with you shortly."

"Oh, thank you, Officer Luck."

Taking the seat opposite mine, she tilted her head down, allowing her brown hair to swing slightly in front of her face. She placed a manilla folder in between us and opened it while strategically positioning it in front of her mouth. As she shuffled papers, she started to speak again.

"The audio for the camera in this room is malfunctioning," she said as her eyes flicked to mine conspiratorially. "Do not acknowledge that I'm speaking to you because the visual is still recording us." She paused and took my silence as my answer. "I had to talk to you before they did. Cody Mason admitted to dating Heather prior to his and Alison's meeting. He also—"

Officer Luck stopped talking half a second before the door opened.

"Officer Luck, you're already here," said the same smelly officer who'd questioned me before.

"Yes, sir, I thought I'd get a head start on setting up the recorder," she said while getting up from the chair and walking to the corner of the room.

"Thank you." He turned his attention toward me. "Ah, Miss Carpenter." The heavy-set officer took his seat across from me. The heavy-set officer took the seat across from me. He still smelled the same—sour and sweaty. As he sat down, you could almost see the smell coming off him. That shit got pushed directly into my awaiting nostrils. Nothing could stop the cringe that settled on my face.

"Officer Cain has informed us that you ran because you were scared. She filled us in, so let's just skip the part of me telling you how that was a poor decision, and we can move straight to the point."

Well then. "Sounds good to me, sir."

"I know you were informed that Cody Mason's fingerprints were a match for those found on the murder weapon."

I nodded.

"Did that come as a surprise to you, Miss Carpenter?"

"Yes, it did."

"Why is that?"

"I don't understand why Cody would have killed Heather. They didn't know each other." I fought the urge to glance at Officer Luck. She'd just finished telling me that

Heather and Cody dated. Of course, I wasn't aware of that before two minutes ago, and I was still in shock over it. Why hadn't Heather told me? That must have been why she stopped hanging out with me when Alison and I became friends. When I'd told Heather how weird Cody had made me feel the first time we'd met, she didn't even blink an eye. She just listened to my story as if she had no idea who I was talking about.

"You're wrong."

"Excuse me, sir?"

"Cody Mason and Heather Dunn dated last year, according to Cody."

Thankfully, the shock on my face was genuine.

"I see you were not aware of their relationship?"

"No, sir. Heather never mentioned Cody."

"When did you first meet Cody Mason?"

"About five months ago? Alison introduced me to him and her friends about a month after she and I met."

"What is the nature of your relationship with Cody Mason?"

"Cody was in our friend group. Like I said, I've known him for about five months."

"How would you describe your relationship with Cody?"

Could I really say I thought he was a douchebag? That I thought he wasn't good enough for Alison? That he'd always made me uncomfortable? I wasn't sure where this line of questioning was going.

"We were friends. We hung out a handful of times in our friend group."

"Did you ever spend time alone with him?"

"No, sir, never."

The officer rifled through some papers. The interrogation seemed to have ended; however, he continued.

"When was the last time you saw Alison Villareal?"

"Right before she left for her work trip to New York. I stayed with her until I could go back to my condo. Oh, sorry, I'm sure you knew that."

"Yes, we did."

"What was the nature of your relationship with Miss Villareal?"

"She was my best friend," I replied, voice cracking. "What—"

"Sir? May I ask how she died? No one has told me." I hated to interrupt the officer, but the question had been boring its way through me, and it spilled out between my teeth before I could stop myself.

"Oh, Miss Carpenter, I see you've not been informed."

"Informed of what?"

"The body that was found and identified as Alison Villareal was a missing Jane Doe. Her body was in such a state when we discovered her that identification was difficult. But when her autopsy was performed, the forensic team discovered the error."

"What are you saying?"

"Miss Villareal is still a missing person."

I gasped out loud. "You mean she could be alive, sir? Is that a real possibility? Did you ask Cody if he knew where she was?"

"Yes, there is a possibility that she is still alive. I cannot discuss it further with you. What I can say is that we have not ruled out your involvement in either Miss Dunn's or Miss Villareal's cases. For all we know, you and Cody Mason conspired together to kill both victims."

"You can't be serious. Sir, you just said you thought Alison was alive, and you cannot possibly think—"

"Miss Carpenter. Since you're now a flight risk, you will be held here without bail until your trial. The simple fact remains that you do not have an alibi for the night of Miss Dunn's murder. By your own admission, you were inside the premises at the time of her death. And as far as Miss Villareal's disappearance goes, you are the last known person to see her alive."

Shit. Shit. Shit. He was right. Fuck, even with Cody looking guilty as hell, they did still have evidence against me. Fuck.

"There is also the matter of your shoes and the bloody footprints."

Fuck, I knew they were going to bring up those damn shoes again. Had I really thought they wouldn't keep me here if I came in for questioning? I was so naïve, so hopeful. I knew I was smarter than this, I just couldn't seem to get a footing on this situation.

Would Officer Luck inform Haywood that I'd be having an extended stay in prison? Well, whatever he wanted me for would have to wait. Hopefully, whoever hired him to investigate this murder would encourage him to continue. I needed all the help I could get. I couldn't be stuck here forever.

"Miss Carpenter, I'm sure you remember how this goes. You'll now be escorted to your cell."

The force of his words hit me like a freight train. Fear slammed into my sternum and fractured my semblance of calm. My hands grasped the metal of my chair so hard that I knew there would be indents on my palms. The room got so cold I swore I could see my breath in front of me.

"Miss Carpenter," Officer Luck said as her hand touched my shoulder. Her proximity comforted me. The warmth of her hand seeped into my skin, allowing me to calm down. I blinked up at her, and I knew she could see my panic, my fear. Her eyes peered back at me through her glasses, and she seemed to be trying to communicate with me.

It will be okay. I will call Haywood. Try to trust us. We will make sure you are okay.

I'm scared.

I know. I'll be here. It's going to be okay; I promise.

I must be going crazy again. This place really had that effect on me, but I could have sworn I heard her in my head.

Another officer walked in and came over to handcuff me. I recognized him as the officer who had walked me to make my phone call to Alison. Great. This guy already hated me, and now I'd evaded the cops and was being held for murder, conspiring to murder, and kidnapping. Ugh. I was in deep shit.

"Told ya you'd be back," he said to me under his breath so quietly that I didn't think anyone else could hear him.

I didn't answer him though. He led me to the same room I'd used before to change into the familiar khaki-colored jumpsuit.

It felt so eerily like the first time. I felt as though I was repeating that terrible day. Was I doomed to repeat the day Heather was murdered all over again? Would there be no escape for me?

I found myself standing at the same iron bars as the officer opened the cell door.

The blow to my back landed so fast I could barely register what had just happened. It knocked me so off-kilter that I fell to my knees.

"Get in you piece of trash," the officer said with a hiss.

He'd elbowed me in my back. What the—?

The kick to my side came just as quickly. I doubled over in pain, holding myself in the fetal position. I refused to meet his gaze, refused to let him see the fear that was surely showing in my eyes. I would not break in front of this redneck asshole.

"Trash like you should stay locked up. You think you're too good to get locked up in a place like this, huh? That you can kill someone and run free? You're in for a rude awakening, girly. I said before, you'd be back, and here ya are. You'll stay here too, and you'll get no special treatment neither. Your friend Officer Cain was removed from your case and was forced to take a few weeks' vacation for helping you."

I winced. The possibility that Officer Cain could get in trouble for coming to get me hadn't even occurred to me. I couldn't respond. The blow to my back had knocked the wind out of me, and my ribs hurt. I just hoped he'd leave.

"Just wait till lights out, girly. You made us look a fool when you hightailed it out of town. You'll be gettin' our thanks for that later," he promised as he slammed the cell door shut and locked it.

I stayed on the floor tightly gripping my body. I was frozen with fear.

Lights out had already been an awful experience. I'd lost part of myself the last time I was here and hadn't regained it back yet. What more could I lose this time around?

I realized that the floor underneath my head was damp. I was crying, sobbing. I couldn't stop the dam that had broken inside of me, so I just kept crying while rocking myself gently on the floor.

"Clarke! ... CLARKE!" Alison's voice broke through the darkness, and I saw her. She was right in front of me. If I reached out, I could touch her. We were in a cavern. No, we were in an underground dungeon that looked like someone had carved it into the side of a mountain.

Alison was behind black bars, her hands extended toward me. I ran to her and took her hands in mine. She looked terrible. Alison always looked polished and beautiful. She'd never had a day when she didn't look fabulous. Her appearance now was jarring.

"Alison, I'm here. I'm here. I thought ... everyone thought you were dead. Where are we?"

"I know, girl, but I'm here, and you've got to come get me. She won't let me leave, Clarke. She lied to me. She—you have to come, Clarke. It's the only way. She'll let me go then. I know it."

"Alison, wait, what? Who is 'she'? What are you talking about?"

"This is real, Clarke," she said, squeezing my hands tighter. Her eyes were wide and bloodshot. Her hair was a mess of tangles, and she was covered in soot. The stench from her cell reached me.

"Alison, have you been here the whole time? Can you tell me where you are? Who has you? Did Cody put you here?"

"Cody? No, girl, what the hell are you talking about? He has nothing to do with this. Fuck Cody. Clarke, you have to get me out of here! No—you're leaving—don't, Clarke! It's not what you think. I was wrong. I'm so sorry. Shit!"

"Alison?"

"Clarke, I'm in Telera—"

I blinked my eyes open. The desperation in Alison's voice clung to me as I realized that I was waking up. No, no, no! I needed to go back! Alison was just about to tell me something about where she was being held. Was she trying to reach me? What had she said? Telera? What the hell was that? No, get a grip, Clarke. It was just a dream. Alison couldn't really communicate with me that way … but … but it just felt so real. I could still feel her hands holding and squeezing mine. I could still smell her stench from being in that awful place for days.

I must have fallen asleep on the floor when I was crying. My temples ached like they always did when I cried before falling asleep, and my body felt sore and battered. Thankfully, it wasn't lights out yet. I still had time to ready myself for that. Hopefully, another officer would come to check on me or something, and I could tell them what had happened. Officer Luck had said to trust her. She said she'd be watching out for me, right? I had to believe her. I needed to believe her.

I pushed myself off the floor and dusted myself off. I took a seat on the bed and looked around.

The trauma of being back here had to have caused that dream. I was projecting, imagining Alison locked up somewhere this whole time.

Well, no more dreams for me. I'd be staying wide awake through lights out. If that officer was coming back to do whatever the hell else, I'd be ready for him. I tucked my knees to my chin, holding my legs with my arms and bringing my feet to rest on the bed, and waited.

When the lights went out, my pulse spiked. I didn't want to be afraid of this asshole. I tried to be strong, but I didn't have a weapon or anything. I only had myself to fight him back. I was pretty sure I had a massive bruise on my back and right side where he'd elbowed and kicked me. Still, I kept my eyes wide, straining to see anything, even though all I saw was darkness.

When the door to my cell creaked open, I legit almost pissed myself. I moved to get off the bed, so I could get into some sort of defensive position.

"Clarke?" Haywood whispered.

"Haywood? Holy shit, Haywood!" I cried. I felt my face dampen. I was crying again. Well, I guess once that dam broke, I'd be crying a lot more now.

He pulled me into him and held me close. His warm body encompassed mine, comforting me, quieting the tremors of fear. My body shook in his arms as I sobbed uncontrollably. I was so relieved. He said he'd see me after I got out, but Luck must have told him what happened.

"Shh, *alcam mae* … you're okay now. You're safe."

"Alca what? Haywood, how are you here?" I blubbered.

"Luck" was his only response.

"Come with me," he said as he took my hand and led me out of the cell.

He then held me closer to him. My feet came off the ground, and the wind whipped quickly through my hair. Did he just pick me up and haul ass? Holy shit, he was fast.

"Haywood, how are we going to get out of here?" I whispered in his ear.

"Simple. We walk out the back door," he said calmly and surely. I chuckled into his hair as I curved myself further into his body. He was crazy, and I'd missed him. I decided to let myself sink into the comfort of his arms around me.

As a door in front of us opened, light from the alley's streetlamp illuminated the otherwise dark corridor. Officer Luck was on the other side.

"Hurry, sir. Go this way. No one will see you. Your car is at the end of this alley."

"Luck, thank you so much," I managed to say before Haywood hurried us toward the car.

"I can walk, you know," I said, but I didn't let go of my hold around Haywood's neck.

"Of course, you can, but I am much quicker than you this way."

"I noticed."

He smiled at me and tightened his hold around my waist. I winced, and his face hardened.

"What's wrong, Clarke? Are you hurt? I felt something earlier tonight but wasn't sure."

"What do you mean, you felt something?"

"Oh, just that I had a bad feeling and knew we needed to expedite our plan to get you free of that place."

"It's nothing, really," I assured him. "You may not have noticed, but I'm a bit clumsy, and I tripped over my feet and fell. I must have bruised something. Those holding cell floors are harder than they look." The lie came to me quickly, and I hoped he'd bought it. The last thing I needed was for Haywood to run back into the prison to avenge me or something. We were in deep enough shit as it was.

"I'll take a look at it when we get to our destination then."

When we reached the car, he deposited me in the passenger side seat and buckled my seatbelt.

"We need to go somewhere, and I need you to trust me, Clarke."

"Yeah, I figured we wouldn't just chill here waiting to be arrested," I replied sarcastically. "You just busted me out of jail. I trust you, Haywood. I couldn't have stayed there. They were going to—" I cleared my throat. "I just needed to get out."

"They were going to do what, Clarke?"

"Nothing, sorry, my head's a bit groggy. I don't even remember what I was going to say."

"Okay … you're acting strangely."

"Oh!" I interrupted. "Could we stop by my place before we go … wherever you have planned? I understand if it's too dangerous, but I really, really don't want to go into hiding without …"

"Without what, Clarke?"

"There's a necklace. It's the only thing of my mom's I have left, and well, she gave it to me before she died."

"Of course, I understand the importance of something like that. I think that it should be okay if we make it a quick trip. I'll park in the back, and you can go in the back door. The police are no longer processing the crime scene where Heather died, and the press has all moved on to harassing Cody."

"That's great, Haywood. Thank you. This means everything to me."

CHAPTER 19

Haywood parked in the alleyway behind my condo and handed me a hoodie.

"There shouldn't be anyone around, but pull the hood up so no one sees your face," he instructed.

I put the hoodie on and pulled it over my head to shield my face in case anyone was walking through the alley. It also helped hide most of the khaki prison-issued jumpsuit.

I walked down the familiar alley behind my condo, pulled out my key, and unlocked the back door. Feeling very much like a burglar, instead of feeling like I'd walked into my own condo, I walked down the hallway, pausing at the same hall closet to grab a flashlight like I had the night I'd found Heather dead.

I reached in and found what I was looking for. I switched it on, and it illuminated the space before me as I continued to creep through my old home.

I walked up the stairs and found my mother's necklace exactly where I'd left it on my nightstand. I was struck by the beauty of it; its memory paled in comparison to the real thing. It had a red star ruby in the center with smaller red gems orbiting around it attached by diamond studs, almost in the shape of a star, with a delicate gold chain. As I secured it around my neck, I took stock of the surrounding room. It looked like someone had turned the place upside down and shaken it. Clothes were everywhere. I grabbed a duffle and shoved a few things quickly inside. Might as well get some shoes and some changes of clothing, and a couple of my favorite books too. I paused at my wall decorated with pictures from the last year and decided to pull down a few to toss in my bag, as well as a picture of my mom and me. It was my favorite picture of the two of us; we looked more like sisters than mother and daughter.

I felt lighter as I walked downstairs, like someone had lifted a weight from my shoulders. The unknown was waiting for me out there, possibly life as a fugitive doing god knew what with Haywood. There was no real plan as far as I knew. But I was free, and I had my most prized possession around my neck and close to my heart. I felt closer to my mom at that moment and felt comforted. I wished she was with me. She would have made me feel safe like she always did. She would say something to make everything make sense again. She would center me.

But she wasn't here. I had to do those things for myself now. And I would. A calmness and strength settled in my core. As I opened the back door to my condo, I turned back and looked down the dark hallway again.

"Goodbye, little condo … goodbye, Heather." My heart ached at the loss of my roommate. I refused to acknowledge Alison's status. She had to be alive somewhere. Maybe Haywood would help me find her.

I walked outside and shut and locked the door. As I turned to walk back toward Haywood, searing pain radiated through my skull, and then everything went black.

CHAPTER 20

Haywood

I felt Clarke's fear spike, so I threw open the car door and dashed down the alleyway. "Clarke!" I yelled. "Clarke!" She didn't answer me as I called for her. When I reached the back door to her condo, I smelled her blood and the same male that I had scented when I found the murder weapon. Cody. Cody had been there, and … the blood I smelled was Clarke's. She must have been injured. I peered around the empty alleyway and saw nothing, not a trace … until I detected faint dragging marks exiting the opposite side of the dirty alleyway. My heart leaped with hope. She had to be okay. I would find her and dispose of this Cody once and for all, consequences be damned. I ran toward the end of the alley to follow the trail where it ended. She must have been put into a car. Finding her on foot would take forever, so I headed back through the alleyway to my car. I could still feel her, so she had to be close, maybe the warehouse district just outside of the city center.

Moments went by as I wound through the city streets toward the warehouse district. Many of them were abandoned, and dreadfully, I understood why Cody would take her out here. This district was all but deserted; she could yell for help, but her cries would go unheard.

He was going to kill her. I had to hurry. The trail ended near one of the more rundown buildings. It was vast; I had to rely on smell to sense her now. She hadn't left a blood trail, which meant the wound he'd inflicted at the condo wasn't fatal. I had to remain positive. She needed me, and I would not fail her—*must* never fail her.

What I smelled as I entered the dark expanse of the warehouse turned my blood to ice. Obscurus. Here? What in the absolute *amiburro* was going on? Was an Obscurus at the head of this crazy situation? Did they orchestrate the murders of Clarke's friends to weed her out somehow? What was their endgame?

I had no time to ponder it further as I raced through the warehouse, desperate to find Clarke.

CHAPTER 21

Clarke

I had the distinct feeling of being dragged across rough terrain. Then I recognized the uneven rhythm of riding in a car as my semiconscious body shifted along with the bumpy road. When the car stopped, I was plucked up and thrown over someone's shoulder, carried inside a building—I assume based on the light change I perceived through my eyelids—and placed on a chair.

My eyes fluttered, as I struggled to open them. I felt as though someone had shoved an ice pick through my right temple. I winced as the light from the bare bulb dangling overhead made my headache worsen. Every muscle in my body twinged like someone had taken a baseball bat to every square inch. My mouth felt so tight, and I couldn't move it. Holy shit, my mouth was duct-taped shut! As the feeling returned to my limbs, I realized my hands and feet were also bound. Acid filled my mouth, and I struggled to breathe through my nose as fear took hold.

How long was I out? Days? Hours? Where the fuck was I? Who hit me? Where was Haywood?

I looked around the dark room. If I had to guess, I was in one of the old, derelict warehouses just outside the city. I seemed to be in some abandoned office room. I was sitting in a broken computer chair, and aged desks were propped against the opposite wall. Pools of dank-smelling water scattered the floor, and it seemed like the light above me was the only one on in the warehouse. Who would bring me here, and why?

Something moved into my line of sight, blocking the light. My vision was blurry, but it cleared enough for me to realize a person was standing in front of me. They were backlit, so their face remained unclear.

"I see you're finally awake. Not so hot now, are you, Clarke?"

Ice filled my veins as I realized exactly who was standing in front of me.

"Cody?" I mumbled incoherently through the duct tape.

"Oh, my manners must have escaped me," he said mockingly before I felt him rip the tape from my face, taking a layer of my skin with it. But the burning feeling on my face was eclipsed by the raw feeling of panic and fear churning in my chest and gut.

"Fuck, Cody! What are—how? Why am I here? Why did you hit me?" My thoughts and questions came out in spurts. I wasn't thinking clearly. I felt like a connection had been severed somewhere in my brain, and I was so cold. Wherever we were, it was freezing. My teeth chattered both in an attempt to warm myself and, embarrassingly, out of fear. Cody had likely killed Heather. He probably had something to do with Alison going missing. Was I moments away from my own death? It couldn't end like this. My life could not be over so soon; I had so much more living to do.

I heard the unmistakable cock of a gun and felt its cold bite on my already-pounding temple. I could no longer breathe.

"You are here, Clarke, because I'm in this stupid fucking mess because of you." His voice raised an octave as if he was trying to yell at me, but he didn't want to be too loud, as if he didn't want anyone to overhear us. Was the warehouse not empty?

I started to scream for help but remembered that a gun was pressed to my head and thought better of it.

"I didn't kill anyone, and we both know you have something to do with this, so"—he opened up a phone and held it in front of my face—"we are going to make a little video where you're gonna confess that you killed Heather and hid Alison somewhere. Then I'm gonna send this to the cops, so they'll arrest you and drop these phony charges they got on me. Your little disappearing act is all over the news, you know. Thanks for that, by the way. It'll make it so much easier to prove you're guilty. People who run have something to hide, Clarke. I would've pegged you for being smarter than that."

"You're crazy," I managed to say through clenched teeth.

Cody shoved the gun harder into my temple as it throbbed. "Shut up, bitch. If you don't do exactly what I say, your brains are going to end up all over this room."

Shit. Shit. Shit. Okay, I needed to think. Haywood was waiting for me. He had to know something was wrong. He'd find me, right? I just had to stall. I had to get Cody to talk. Wasn't that what all criminals did? They loved to monologue, tell their grand plan to the person they were about to kill. I just had to get him going.

"Cody, you're a good guy. You don't want to hurt me." I lied terribly. He was a shitty human being, and I'm pretty sure he knew how I really felt about him. But I was hoping that I'd appealed to his ego just enough. Just enough to buy me time.

"Ha! Good guy? Really, Clarke?" He called me out for my petty attempt at flattery. "My reputation was ruined because of you. Everyone thinks I'm a murderer. Hell, the cops think I killed Heather and that I got Alison stashed somewhere. They even asked if you were going to be my next victim. Ironic, ain't it?" He laughed to himself. "And you can cut the shit. I know you're not my biggest fan. Alison had a big mouth."

"Had? What did you do to her, Cody? Where is she—"

My face stung as Cody backhanded me. In the last few hours, I'd been elbowed in the back, kicked in the ribs, rescued, hit over the head, kidnapped, and now was tied up while desperately trying not to die. Pain was quickly becoming my closest companion.

"Do I really need to put the duct tape back on, Clarke?"

Shit. I was the fucking worst at this. Maybe if I changed tactics …

"Was the hunting knife really yours?"

He blinked in surprise. "Well, it sure looked like a knife I had that went missing a few weeks ago. I told the cops that too, but they didn't wanna listen. Said everyone says that when something that's theirs turns up as a murder weapon."

"They did that to me too."

"Huh? What the hell are you talking about now?"

"They said some shoes Alison bought me, that I only wore one time, matched bloody shoe prints that were found leading out of the condo."

"Fuck …," he said as he seemed to consider our shared plight.

I felt a jolt of hope. He was talking. Stalling was working. Come on, Haywood, wherever you are, please hurry.

"Hey!" He yelled as he rammed the gun deeper still. "We ain't here to talk about your shitty luck and my shitty luck. We're here to record your confession, Clarke, and if you don't, I'm gonna blow your brains out," he slurred. I smelled it then—the unmistakable stench of whiskey sweating through his pores.

"Are you drunk?"

"Duh, I've been drinking. What the hell else would I be doing? I paid my bail, and they sent me home with a stupid ankle monitor. Those things are easy as hell to get off, by the way. I started drinking and thinking. Thinking and drinking, and that's when I came up with this amazing idea. You confess on camera, and I prove I'm innocent. Easy."

Suddenly, a jolt of awareness ran through me. A warmth burned between my breasts, thawing the freezing temperature of the room. I felt a thread in my soul pull taut. I looked up, and my eyes drifted past Cody toward twin sea-green jewels that pierced the darkness and bored into me. Someone was standing in the darkened doorway behind Cody. My eyes adjusted as a face emerged. The jewels were eyes, the most incredible eyes I'd ever seen, belonging to a tall, gorgeous man with dark-brown hair in perfect contrast to his eyes, a strong jawline, furrowed brow, and tensely drawn lips. He was wearing a black leather jacket, a black shirt, jeans, and black combat boots. I was beyond struck by how attractive he was, so much so that I almost forgot that my life was in jeopardy. The stranger lifted his index finger to his pursed lips, signaling me to stay quiet, and I obeyed.

I fixed my eyes on Cody instead, not wanting to draw attention to my would-be savior. That's why he had to be here, right? He was going to help me. There was no way he was a coconspirator with Cody. He wasn't part of the crew. However, something about him gave me the weirdest sense of déjà vu. Maybe Haywood sent him?

Determined to keep Cody distracted, I decided to play along with his plan for having me confess on video. If it bought me time, it'd be worth it.

"Okay."

"Okay?" Cody questioned.

"If you promise not to hurt me, I'll say whatever you want me to say."

"See, I knew you'd see things my way," he said as he took a knife out of his pocket and freed my bound hands and feet. "Can't have you looking like you're all tied up making this video, right? I'm glad you are finally understanding the situation you're in. Someone like you just needed the proper motivation," he said as the hand not holding the gun skated up the side of my torso. He grabbed me and pulled me flush to him. The hard length of his arousal pressed into my belly, and bile filled my throat.

"What the—?"

"Shh …." His breath oozed with alcohol as it hung hot and heavy between us. I turned my head and tried not to breathe in any of it. Then he started to sloppily caress the underside of my right boob. Icy fear and fiery rage zipped up my spine as nausea turned my stomach. I was going to throw up.

One moment Cody was in front of me, and the next, he just disappeared. Poof. I blinked and then realized that jewel eyes had tackled him. He was trying to wrestle the gun from Cody. Movement in the doorway drew my gaze.

"Clarke!" Haywood yelled my name as he burst into the room.

CHAPTER 22

Haywood

Warm light cascaded from an open door. I vaulted through the opening and screamed her name.

"Clarke!"

My eyes connected with hers, and raw terror gazed back at me. I felt elation spike as she saw I was here to rescue her. Her expression quickly switched to a bone-chilling alarm.

I had but a second to realize my folly. In my haste to find her, I'd made a colossal mistake. I failed to acquaint myself with my surroundings before I announced my presence.

There were two men on the floor wrestling with a firearm. One was the Obscurus, and the other … Cody.

I would kill this human cruelly and without mercy.

CHAPTER 23

Clarke

The two men on the ground whipped their heads toward Haywood. Cody took that moment of distraction to aim the gun at me.

Jewel eyes and Haywood screamed my name in unison.

I felt the fiery entry of the bullet before I heard the shot ring out like a death bell.

I looked down at where my hand was flush with my abdomen. My hand fell open as a dark red and warm wetness started pouring through my fingers and flowing down my body. I looked up to see jewel eyes twist Cody's neck in an unnatural position. The last thing I heard was the sickening crunch of his neck snapping. The last thing I saw was Cody's body falling limply to the floor. My nostrils filled with the pungent smell of my blood mixed with the dank, mildew smell of the warehouse. My vision turned black, and then I felt nothing at all.

CHAPTER 24

Haywood

I ran to her, bypassing the Obscurus, who made quick work of ending Cody's life. I couldn't care less; I just needed her in my arms. She had to be okay.

"Clarke, *mae*, please wake up." I rocked her gently as I brought my hand to her cheek.

I turned to the Obscurus and realized I knew him. Lachlan. Osiria's right hand. What was the emissary of the dark fae doing here, and why was he trying to save Clarke? No matter. Clarke needed healing, and that was one thing I wasn't capable of doing. I would beg or barter anything for his service. Obscurus had unique and powerful healing skills.

When I asked for his help, he didn't hesitate to oblige but needed to do so in Teleran, where his magic was at its strongest. As her heartbeat thumped weakly, I opened a portal and took my enemy and the girl I loved to my manor home in Teleran. I held her tightly as blood sputtered from her mouth as a sickening, wet noise escaped her lips. No, it couldn't be too late. I would not accept her death.

CHAPTER 25

Clarke

Death was like floating on a weightless cloud, or like being hugged tightly and gently at the same time. It felt like I was floating in a shallow ocean, and instead of the fear I normally felt when submerged in water, I had a sense of safety. I couldn't open my eyes. Maybe we couldn't see in the afterlife? At this point, I couldn't force myself to feel concerned. I was too at peace.

I couldn't feel my body anymore, but I wasn't afraid. I'd always imagined our souls as vibrant beings encased in a prison of skin. That when our bodies fail us at the time of death, we are set free, no longer confined, no longer in a constant state of entropy. I did, however, have the weirdest sensation of still breathing.

I'd always felt the act of breathing was a magical thing anyway. Scientists said it's one of those involuntary motor functions of the body, but I don't know. I always felt that it was a way to center my soul, my being, to become one with the energy and air around me, calm and quiet like my mom had taught me. So it only made sense that, now that I was free of my constraints, breathing remained.

The ascent into feeling was strange. It came on slowly. First came a slight tremor that felt like water was leaking from my body, a cold flare here and there, and then a dull vibrating twitch reverberated through me. Then, as if my nervous system was still intact, I felt a thousand neurons firing off at once, like a lightning storm exploding on my insides. Pain flowed through me like lava. I had a distinct feeling that when the lava settled, when it cooled and hardened, I'd become something solid, something different.

A fluttering feeling gave me the impression that I must still have eyes. And I must have because they slowly peeled open. Bright and beautiful light poured into them, into me, and I was looking up at a ceiling of sorts. It was circular and glass, and I could see the most fantastic sky through it. Swirls of pinks, blues, and greens painted such a breathing taking scene that my eyes blurred. I was crying. Did tear ducts still work when you died? That's … well, that was weird.

Slowly, my sense of the space around me became more corporeal. I wasn't in the clouds or being hugged softly. I was in a bed, the most luxurious I'd ever seen, surrounded by the textiles of the gods. I couldn't move anything except my eyes, but out of the right corner of them, I saw a familiar face.

Haywood.

His blonde hair was untethered and laid in messy waves around his shoulders. He looked pained as dark circles underlined his eyes. Was Haywood dead too? No. He seemed too real. Too sad.

I blinked rapidly as my breath became labored and my heart knocked loudly against my chest. I could feel sweat dripping from my brow. Okay, I really expected not to sweat after dying. Something was off.

"It's okay, Clarke. You're going to be okay," he said as he came to kneel beside the bed. He took my hand and pressed a kiss to my knuckles.

My hand? I still had hands. Wait. I … I … I was not dead. How? Cody shot me. There was so much blood. I felt my heart slow and stop. Didn't I? How was this possible?

"I know you have a lot of questions, but right now, I need you to rest and get better," Haywood responded to me as if he could sense my thoughts, my questions. His kiss lingered on my knuckles as the feeling in my limbs slowly returned.

I heard a throat clear and let my eyes drift to the opposite side of the room.

Jewel eyes.

He tucked a shaggy black curl behind his ear and gave me a small smile.

As our eyes locked, I couldn't seem to catch my breath. Haywood squeezed my hand tighter.

"Clarke," jewel eyes said as he came closer to where I lay on the bed, "it's very nice to meet you. I'm Lachlan."

Loch Ness? Um, like the place with the monster?

A chuckle left his lips, and I realized I said that part out loud.

My cheeks heated as he took the hand Haywood wasn't holding into his. Fire erupted through me from his contact, goosebumps pebbled my skin, and a flash of something I couldn't quite put into words entered my mind. Familiar. Right.

His eyes widened, and his eye brows flew upwards. Something like recognition and surprise filled his gaze as he said, "It's you." His tone sounded so bewildered that I almost didn't realize what he'd said.

"What's me?" I barely squeaked out.

I felt it then. A whooshing behind my eyes. A low buzz of energy beneath my skin. It almost seemed like I could peel back that first layer and see it swirling, flowing, and coursing through my veins. It was like waking up from a deep sleep. My body was groggy with mortality, and as I stretched and tossed the blanket of sleep back, this new me began to slough out of the shell it was encased in, awakening into something magnificent. I was awake. Awake and made new.

CHAPTER 26

Lachlan

I could hardly believe the truth looking me directly in the eye. She was real? This siren had haunted my dreams for months. And now Osiria had sent me to fetch her from the human world? Did this have anything to do with the prophecy? Just an hour ago, I'd been rolling the old scroll through my fingertips over and over as I contemplated its meaning.

Down the line, centuries untold,
death and destruction will unfold.
To prevent this awful fate,
unlikely halves must part from hate.
From clasping hands of mortal foes,
power sang of fate to be sowed.
For peace and prosperity,
for love, joy, and destiny,
a descendant of both their powers,
will forfeit heart and increase hours.

What in the actual *amiburro*? It had to be the most asinine thing I'd ever read. I'd need to take it to one of Alternae, the elders of Teleran, to see if they could make sense of the riddle. To me, it was utter nonsense.

I didn't want to part with it so quickly though. I wasn't ready to take it to my mistress and let her know that I'd likely found the way to save Teleran. It had to be that stupid prophecy for which both sides of our world had been searching; however, I could not shake the feeling that I should keep it to myself.

When my sovereign returned to us from her travels to the human world, she'd changed. No one noticed her subtle tells except me. She'd seemed as though her skin was pulled too tight for our world. Her heart … well, she had one. Quite the shift from the Osiria we all knew and feared.

In her absence, she left me to serve as regent. I must say, ruling suited me far more than I could've imagined. Although I would never betray my sovereign, I was reluctant to hand the reins back to her when she returned.

The scent of her power invaded my nostrils, warning me she was near.

"Lachlan?" She beckoned me as she rounded the hallway and came into view.

She was striking, my sovereign. Black waves cascaded down her back, over her shoulders, and settled at her waist. Her eyes were perfect twins to her hair, black as night. When she was angry, they would glow like two coals set aflame. Her height made even the strongest male cower. She was strength; she was poise; she was stunning. I feared her as much as I loved her.

"There you are. I've been summoning you for an hour now. You know how I hate to be kept waiting."

I got up from the desk where I'd been dissecting the riddle I'd found, shuffling my papers to hide it, and turned to fully face Osiria.

"I'm sorry, my sovereign. I was distracted with preparations for Altfevis. I didn't feel your pull until just now." Altfevis was an annual festival that took place at the border of both sides of Teleran. Once a year, we gathered in peace and gorged ourselves to the point of death. It was an attempt at tranquility by our two sovereigns to keep us from warring and fighting.

"Ah … well, next time, do pay more attention."

"Yes, my sovereign," I said, bowing with a flourish.

"I need you to do something for me, but I will need to bind you from repeating what I'm about to tell you."

"Of course, my sovereign, I'm ever your humble servant."

"Good, reach out your hand."

She took a gilded dagger from the sheath hidden under the bustle of her gown and split open the palm of my hand.

As blood began to bead and pool, she repeated the slice on her own palm.

"I bind you, Lachlan, in trust and in duty, not to share in word or deed anything you think, see, feel, or hear regarding Clarke Carpenter to anyone other than me, lest you die a suffocating and horrible death." She took her bloody hand and joined it with my own.

"I swear it, my sovereign," I said as an uncomfortable sting traveled up my arm, sealing our deal.

She took a cloth from the satchel at her side and cleaned her hand and dagger free of blood, and then extended it to me to clean my own cut.

"Sovereign, if I may be so bold, who is Clarke Carpenter?"

"Clarke is a female in the human world. She thinks she is human, but she is not. She is fae and is under our protection, as she is an Obscurus."

I wondered if she could see my shock. If she did, her face gave nothing away. I wasn't aware we still had fae left in the human world. I thought the atmosphere alone was too toxic for our kind to survive long-term. I made sure my face was impassive and calm as she continued.

"As she is under our protection, I need you to go and retrieve her. She has gotten herself into some trouble, and I fear the worst. You must rescue her and bring her back here, straight to me. Do not be seen by anyone else."

"It will be done, my sovereign. When must I go?"

"Now, immediately, in fact."

"Of course, I will pack my provisions imminently. How will I find her?"

"I will allow you to feel her power signature so that you will be able to track her."

"Sovereign, how can this be? I thought that was only for mated fae or—"

"Do you doubt my abilities, Lachlan?"

"No, my sovereign, forgive me, of course not," I quickly responded, lowering my head again.

"She believes herself to be human, so you mustn't scare her. Bring her here by force if you must, but do not harm her. Try to keep any explanations vague. Let me do the explaining once she is with me."

"Yes, my sovereign."

"And, Lachlan, do not fail me, or this will be your last task. Are we clear?"

"Yes, my sovereign."

"Take caution. Clarke is … special. You may run into other fae seeking her out."

"Other Obscurus?"

"No, I have reason to believe an Estival is close to her."

"Why would—"

"Remember your place, Lachlan."

"Yes, forgive me, my sovereign."

Without another word, she walked to my credenza where decanters of various liquids sat atop a tray alongside a selection of glassware. Taking a wine goblet in one hand, she squeezed her injured hand until blood dripped down into the glass. Filling the rest of the goblet with water, she held out the pinkish liquid toward me.

"Drink this, and it will connect you to Clarke. Follow her signature and find her, Lachlan."

I dutifully took the goblet and tipped its contents down my throat. A coppery sweetness flowed past my taste buds before I swallowed.

I could feel the blood travel through my body, first warming my belly and then flowing all the way to my fingers and toes. I felt a tightening at my core, like an invisible string tugging me toward this mysterious Clarke.

"Can you feel her?"

"Yes, my sovereign."

"Good. Well, what are you waiting for? We do not have time to waste."

"At once, my sovereign." I would have pled for her dismissal anyway. As soon as that heat flared to life, I felt an overwhelming need to get to Clarke as soon as possible.

Excruciating pain from the back of my head brought me to my knees.

"Arise at once, Lachlan," she commanded.

"My sovereign?" I questioned while bringing my hand to inspect the wound that was surely splitting my skull in half.

"You'll find no blood, Lachlan. This is the result of the blood and binding. You can now feel her—her emotions, her pain, mental and physical."

"Then she was just struck, my sovereign."

"Run, Lachlan, as fast as you can. Save her. If someone has caused her harm or if you run into any Estival opposition, you know what to do."

Racing toward the closet portal to Earth, I launched myself through. A panicked thought crossed my mind: What would happen if this Clarke were killed? Would our connection stop my heart as well? I steeled myself against further such thoughts, as they would only cloud and confuse me.

The portal deposited me in a city. The absence of my full magic was like a weight on my chest, which almost crippled me until I felt the powerful tug again. I followed the feeling like crumbs through the forest.

I reached an old, seemingly abandoned building, and the connection throbbed. She's here. She must be here.

I followed the sound of raised voices to a room spilling muted orange light into the dark warehouse.

The door to the orange-lit room stood ajar, and I slowly filled the entryway.

Lightning seemed to hit me in the chest as two of the most beautiful eyes stared back at me in fear. Her eyes widened. Did she feel it too?

I raised my finger to my mouth to signal her silence. Then I took in the other person in the room—a male with shaggy blonde hair shoved a cell phone in Clarke's face before he freed her hands and pulled her body into his. Her fear and disgust were palpable.

Flames almost shot out of my fingers as I saw him put the cold metal barrel of a gun to her temple as he stroked her body with his grimy hand.

Mine. The thought rose suddenly from the depths of my mind. *No one harms what is mine.* A primal need to protect her took over my body, and I launched myself at her captor without a thought.

The male was shockingly strong and smelled of liquor. When our eyes met, I saw a wild determination in them. He was crazed. I was surprised to find how much weaker I was on Earth. Normally, I should've been able to snap this human like a twig.

I almost had the weapon in my hand when someone else burst through the doorway.

"Clarke!" a familiar voice yelled.

The outburst momentarily distracted me, and a shot rang out.

To my horror, Clarke grasped her wounded stomach, and her eyes filled with terror. Because of the link Osiria imbued in me, I could feel Clarke's immense pain. I almost doubled over but remained upright. She thought she was dying. It felt like she might be right. Perhaps I would die here beside this human. It would be fitting. I was charged with her safety and failed utterly. Osiria did not abide failure, and frankly, neither did I.

My self-pity receded as determination took root. I would save her. I would not fail. Anger welled up inside me, fueling my strength. A fury I'd never known before took over my body, and all I could think of was punishing and destroying anyone who hurt this female.

I looked down at the male who shot Clarke, took his head into my hands, and twisted. His neck popped, severing his spinal cord and extinguishing his life.

Good. Such a waste of blood and bones.

I looked up to see that Clarke was on the floor with a male by her side. He was calling her name and caressing her face. An unnatural sense of possessiveness washed over me. I was wildly jealous of this human man.

No, not a man, I realized. He was an Estival, a particular one whom I knew and loathed. Haywood. He was to his sovereign what I was to mine. What the hell was he doing here? How did he know Clarke? Why did he feel at liberty to touch what was mine?

My need to remove Haywood from Clarke's side momentarily distracted me until the link we shared alerted me to her weakening heartbeat. I rose to go to her as Haywood rose with her in his arms and turned to me.

Anger and irritation flared in his eyes as he recognized me. But then his expression softened.

"Can you save her?" he asked, desperation clinging to his words.

His power may be great, but as an Estival he did not have the power to heal like the Obscurus did. Our power was earth and fire, while theirs was wind and water. With our earth magic came the ability to heal even the most mortal wounds.

"Yes, but we need to take her to Teleran. My magic cannot breathe in this world."

"We can take her to my manor house. You will not be welcome in the palace."

"Fine. Let's go." Normally, I'd have argued with him and demanded we take her to my home instead but there was no time, and I was wary of being close to Osiria. I needed more time with Clarke.

He spoke a phrase in Entera, the language of the fae, and opened a portal to a bedroom lit with an array of colors. The three of us stepped through, and Haywood quickly deposited Clarke on the bed.

I approached her and laid my hands atop her wound. Warm energy pulsed through me as I willed my power to push out the bullet, stitch her skin back together, and pump fresh blood through her body. I lifted my hands only when I felt her heart rate return to a normal cadence. My own heart quieted as well.

I looked up to find Haywood looking back at me with relief and gratitude shining through his eyes. He bowed slightly, and it shocked me.

"I still hate you, and you're going to tell me exactly why you were on Earth trying to save Clarke. But thank you," his voice broke, "thank you for saving her life. I owe you a life debt."

"I didn't do it for you," I replied caustically, "and I don't owe you any explanation, just as you owe me nothing in return."

Clarke stirred on the bed, distracting us both. I quickly wiped her blood from my hands with a rag I found on the nearby shelf. I didn't want to scare her with the sight of it.

Her eyes opened, and magic, so powerful and thick, filled the room. What the—? It felt like ... no, that was not possible.

Haywood walked over to her, took her hand in his, and spoke softly to her.

When her eyes found mine, it wasn't just her beauty that shocked me. I knew her. Not as Clarke, but that face, those lips, her body—I knew it as well as my own. I knew every inch of her, although we'd never met.

I introduced myself and took her other hand in mine. Something in my soul, at my core, pulled tight again, much like when Osiria made it possible for me to follow Clarke's power signature, but stronger, much stronger. It was like a web formed between Clarke and I. Her eyes widened. Did she feel it too? Did she recognize me?

"It's you." The words escaped my lips before I realized what I'd said.

"What's me?" she replied with a groggy voice. Her voice, weak though it was, was like a balm to my soul.

I couldn't respond to her. She didn't understand what was happening between us, but I did. And I was terrified. None of this made sense. Did Osiria know? Who was this female to her? I had so many questions, but all I could focus on were those jade-green eyes looking back at me.

Clarke was my *mae obires*, my mate.

EPILOGUE

I arrived in a wooded area right outside the city just as the sun started to set. Dusk fell quickly.

I was exhausted. I'd spent *two days* procuring a cadaver from the morgue. She was labeled as a Jane Doe, so it wasn't like anyone would miss her. I'd been lucky to find one that had blonde hair like mine, although hers was mangled and matted with blood. Her death had been a gruesome one, and I had to think that the ending I was giving her was far better than her previous one. She would get to end her life as me—the most fabulous Alison Villareal.

I had to spit and rub tons of my DNA on her hoping that it'd be enough to get a positive match for me. Of course, if Daddy chose to have an autopsy, they'd find out quickly that it wasn't me, but I'd be long gone by then. So whatever.

Throwing the body behind the salon where I worked was poetic justice. That place was so far beneath me, and my boss was an asshole. Ideally, they'd receive some bad press, and clients would be too afraid to go there after one of their stylists was brutally murdered. One could only hope. After today, I would never see any of those bitches again.

I felt a small pang of sadness when I thought of Clarke though. I'd really loved her, but she'd come into my life with her sunshine and positivity and enchanted all my friends. Her biggest crime had been putting Cody under her thrall. I suppose it wasn't her fault that she shimmered with a quiet light and brightened every room she entered. We were all just moths to her flame. Even I was inexplicably drawn to her. I adored her and much as loathed her.

She was clueless though. After I'd pinned these two murders on her, she'd rot in prison never illuminating anyone else's world ever again. I'd found an old beat up knife in Cody's garage one morning after I'd spent the night at his house. It made the perfect weapon to kill Heather with, it shoved easily through her ribcage as it pierced her heart. Wearing the shoes I'd bought Clarke for her thirtieth birthday and using them to track Heather's blood out of their condo was methodical. Sneaking into her room while she slept and throwing them in the back of her closet to solidify her guilt, brilliance.

Cody and everyone else would only see her as the villain I'd made her out to be. My truth would be the only truth they would see. I chuckled at my genius. Clarke's light cast shadows on the rest of us, and now she would live the rest of her life in mine.

I couldn't wait to get to Teleran and then ask for Cody to join me. He'd be shocked at first, but then he'd be so impressed by my cleverness that he'd fall more and more in love with me. We'd live in splendor together. I would be his life, his love.

Clarke had tried to take him from me, and for that alone, she deserved her punishment. Fuck Clarke. After this moment, she'd be as dead to me as that cadaver woman who took my place.

Now, on to more present and amazing things. My destiny was waiting for me. I wondered if living in Teleran would make me even prettier?

I looked up and down the tree line searching for the opening as it had been described to me. I almost stumbled past it. The trees bent and twisted into a circular gateway. Well, time to get this show on the road.

The wraith-like creature from my dream instructed me to say some unintelligible words, and apparently a portal to Teleran would open for me. I did as I was told.

Fates muciparous.

The view of the woods beyond the gateway contorted and swirled until a translucent portal, like the surface of a soap bubble, appeared in front of me. The gateway now revealed a world picked straight out of my dreams. Dark skies were accented with red structures that looked like lava flows frozen in time. I approached the portal and took a deep breath before I stepped through.

I had arrived. Finally.

I looked behind me and could see the city, its various buildings forming a crown-shaped skyline. I had no regrets leaving it behind. It always felt much too small for me. I knew I was destined for more.

Snow crunched under my feet as I turned back toward my future. The wraith had given no further instructions, only that I was to cross through. I assumed they would meet me here to gift me with my rewards. I looked around again, clutching my coat closer to my body. It was much cooler than I'd anticipated. I continued to walk while trailing my belongings behind me.

Suddenly, I was grabbed by strong hands that threw my body backward. My head hit a black rock with a crack, and everything went dark and silent.

I woke up in a pit of darkness. My body was frozen through, my coat was missing, and my head throbbed incessantly. I scrambled around on the floor finding it wet and smelling of sulfur. What was going on? My eyes adjusted, and I saw crude black bars in front of me. Beyond the bars, I could see a huge cavern of other cell-like structures like the one I was in. There had to be a mistake. Whoever put me here had no idea who I was.

I called out for help. Whoever discarded me here would pay. I was no one's prisoner!

"No one will be coming for you, dear," a sultry voice answered. I recognized the voice of the wraith, once gravely but now as clear as a bell.

"But, no, I did everything you asked me to do! You promised me—"

"Silence!" The wraith's voiced echoed off the cavernous dungeon. Fear stifled any response I had. "You were a means to end; that's all. And I have honored our agreement. You will live out the rest of your days here in Teleran, and the man you love will die soon, possibly still loving you, so he will only ever love you as he will no longer draw breath."

"What?! No," I sobbed, "please, I wanted to be powerful like you. I wanted to be adored."

The wraith cackled a cruel laugh. "To be powerful, you must be feared, sometimes hated, but mostly you must strike terror in the hearts of others. Love is irrelevant. The powerful are worshiped, which surpasses being 'adored' as you so put it. It is no fault of mine that you are an ignorant, weak human incapable of a decent bargain. And as you are not fae, our bargain was never binding anyway. Be glad you yet breathe. For your crimes, you deserve a knife through your own heart.”

“But … but … you told me to—”

“What I commanded and why is no concern of yours.” The wraith’s footsteps alerted me that they were leaving.

“No! Wait!” I called desperately.

“Such insolence! You dare to command me?” A dark wave of power rippled through the bars choking my air flow. “You will live the rest of your days here as you sought to cause harm to what is mine.”

“No, no, I would never—” My words halted as the air once more evaporated from me. The wraith stepped into the dim light that trickled down through an opening at the peak of the cave. I gasped.

“Clarke?!”

The wraith cackled again as they turned to walk away once more. “What a stupid female you are.”

“Wait, don’t go! What’s going on? You owe me!”

The wraith whipped around quickly, reaching through the bars to grasp my chin tightly with their long, thin fingers. Their sharp nails pierced my skin and drew blood.

“I owe you nothing but your death. You will rot here. No one will come for you. It will be as if you never existed at all.”

The air stilled, and I realized my fate. I’d been tricked. I would die here, and I knew with resounding clarity that Clarke was to blame. Hate took root and filled my mouth with ash. I vowed that if I ever escaped this place, she would pay the price for robbing me of my destiny.

A Note From Carter

Death Rattle was my first novel. I believe we all have a story inside of us, and this one and the wide world of Teleran has been stuck between my two ears since I was a high school student who was in a writer's club- dreaming about writing her first novel.

Life happens fast, sometimes bad, mostly good, and we get busy, we lose our way. It took a pandemic to quite literally pause my life and give me a chance to remember that there were other dreams I had besides the daily grind. Much like Clarke, I was on the eat, grind, sleep spin cycle. This is my own journey and adventure into living a more rounded and fulfilled life full of magic. I hope that you read this book and the ones to come and find a home. I hope you find characters that you can relate to; I hope you find Teleran and its beauty, a place to escape when all the world's sounds become too loud.

If you loved Death Rattle, please consider leaving a review on Amazon or GoodReads. Also, follow us on Instagram @carterpughwrites, on TikTok (carterpughwrites), and sign up for our email updates through our website www.carterpughwrites.com.

About The Author

Carter Pugh lives in North Carolina with her husband and her puppy son, Cheese. She loves reading fantasy, romance, and sci-fi. Writing has been a love and passion for her most of her life, but she didn't start her writing career until 2023 when she published her debut novel, Death Rattle. In her spare time, when she isn't reading or writing, she loves watching British TV shows such as Escape to the Country and Absolutely Fabulous. Carter's family is from England, and she has always shared a deep love for the country and its culture as a result. To learn more about Carter and to follow along for more details on future releases, please follow on Instagram (@carterpughwrites), TikTok (carterpughwrites), or visit her website (carterpughwrites.com).

Acknowledgments

I want to thank, first and foremost, my husband. Three years ago, when I told him (rather out of the blue, I might add) that I was going to write a book, his only response was supportive. He bought me the laptop that I now use to write with. He has been and always will be my number-one fan and supporter. Teleran would not exist without him.

To every friend who said they wanted to read my book and help usher the confidence to continue on, to publish, and to keep creating, I thank you.

To anyone who has cracked open Death Rattle, shared it with your friends, or shared it on social media, I am forever grateful. Thank you for giving my world a chance.

Thank you to my favorite authors, without whom I may not have been inspired at all. Thank you, J. R. R. Tolkien, C.S. Lewis, Sarah J. Mass, Jennifer L. Armentrout, and countless others who have given me worlds that I adore escaping to.

Thank you to the authors I reached out to for advice who kindly wrote me back with great advice and steered me with great direction, Sarah A. Parker and Stacey Marie Brown. Your books and your words have inspired me and warmed my heart.

 And a special thanks to the person whom I feel my gratitude pales in comparison to all you did for me...to my editor, Melisa Graham. Thank you for taking such good care of my debut novel and working with me so diligently

and seamlessly. I cannot thank you enough for helping me
bring Death Rattle to fruition in its finest form.

Glossary Of Terms

Obscurus- dark Fae with the power of fire and earth.
Alternae- the elders of the Fae.
Estival- light Fae with the power of air and water.
Teleran- the realm of the Fae
Lesult- earth
Alfmam- fire magic wielder; Nerites
Cielgas- ice magic wielder; Estival
Enstompian- all powerful
Impestuses- power to regenerate after death
Anet Vireo- magic of both light and dark fae
Mae Obires- mate
Mae- love
Fates muciparous- open up
Incataovitia- prophecy
Rafunto- fate
Lifia- daughter
Tamer- mother
Erpta- father
Alstrum- husband/wife/spouse
Rubiroam, Borurami, Amiburro- fuck, various expletives
Cremtnux- shit
Lucamor- oracle
Furrem Mirots- death by iron and darkness
Juanamira- marijuana
Nivos-wine
Enterna-language of the fae